CW01498110

Hollister Sisters
Mail Order Brides

Books 1-5

Debby Mayne

ISBN-13: 9781718038288

.

Julia's Arranged Marriage

Hollister Sisters
Mail Order Brides

Debby Mayne

The fear of the Lord is the beginning of knowledge: but fools despise wisdom and instruction.
Proverbs 1:7

Chapter 1

(May 1881, Virginia)

"You are not going to town alone," John Hollister commanded before he left for work. "And that is final."

Julia tightened her jaw as she always did, glared at her father for several seconds, and then turned around and stormed out of the room without a word. She could hear her father mumbling something about his obstinate daughter, but she didn't care. People had said much worse about her.

Oh, who was she kidding? She did care, way too much. But ever since Mama died, Julia felt as though all the joy had been taken from the house. Her older sister Lenora who lived on the other side of town was widowed and had one child, so that left Julia in charge when Papa wasn't there. And he wasn't there quite a bit.

Julia's only joy, it seemed, was the rose bush in the side yard. She and Mama had planted it a few months before Mama died, and now she felt as though it represented the good times they once had.

Each bud offered hope—promise for the future. And as each one opened with its glorious white petals, she remembered Mama lovingly stroking them.

After her housework that morning, she rewarded herself

with a trip to the garden where the lonely rose bush had finally started to get its spring leaves. But she'd still spend some time with it since that was also her place of peace and quiet where she could pray and have alone time with God before she had to go back in the house and start supper.

Once back in the house, she opened the pantry door and noticed how little she had to choose from. The only meat they had was a small amount of pork fat, and there were very few jars of beans she'd canned last summer.

She finally decided on lima beans, rice, and cornbread. She'd season the beans with pork and salt. Papa didn't much care for rice, but he knew she used it to make meals stretch.

"You look like you've been sucking lemons, Julia. What on earth is the matter with you?"

Julia glanced up from the counter where she'd laid out all of the ingredients for supper, gave her younger sister Sarah a cursory glance, and shrugged. "Nothing is the matter with me." She looked Sarah up and down. "You are the one who should be talking. Look at you." Julia reached out and spun her sister around. "You look like you've been wallowing in the mud."

Sarah tilted her head back and let out her girlish giggle. "I've been playing with the pastor's little boys, and you know how little boys can be."

"You look more like you've been playing with the pigs. Now go get cleaned up so you can help me put supper on the table."

Sarah groaned. "I don't understand why you are so serious all the time. Can't you relax a little bit and enjoy life?"

"Looks like you've been enjoying life enough for the both of us. Now scoot."

Sarah held up both hands. "Okay, okay. I'll go get cleaned up." She started for the door before coming to an abrupt halt and spinning around to face Julia. "While I'm doing that, you might want to think about doing something about your scowl. It isn't becoming for a lady."

Before Julia had a chance to respond, Sarah took off as though being chased by wild animals. Julia stood there and stared at the door as she thought about what Sarah had said. She knew it was true. Pretty much everyone who cared about her tried to coax a smile, but Julia didn't think much was worthy of smiling for. It was rough being barely twenty and having so much household responsibility for so long.

Mama's death had taken its toll on the family. If Papa had a son, it might not have been so bad. But with four girls— one of them a widowed mother—and all of them strong-willed and with minds of their own, he always seemed perplexed and frustrated.

Julia knew Papa wanted them all married and out of the house. Still, she worried about what would become of him. He worked hard, and yet he still struggled to put food on the table. She couldn't imagine him taking care of himself if he lived alone

Sarah came back out, grinning like a girl who didn't have a care in the world, until Julia shot her a look that was reserved for times when she meant business. "I said go on. What are you doing out here?"

"I just wanted to tell you I saw Papa coming up the road. He looks happy too."

"Papa looks happy?" This Julia had to see. She wiped her hands on the towel and walked over to the side window overlooking the road leading to the house. "You're right. I wonder why."

"What do you mean, you wonder why? It's okay for him to be happy."

"Of course it is. It's just that I haven't seen him smiling for … in a very long time."

They both hovered near the door, waiting for Papa to walk in. As soon as they heard his footsteps on the front porch, Julia backed away, but Sarah flung open the door.

"Papa, you look like you have some good news."

His smile widened as he lifted an envelope. "It's better than good ... it's great!"

Sarah reached for the letter, but he held it higher than she could reach. "Hold your horses there, girlie. This doesn't even pertain to you, although it will affect you later."

"What is it?"

"You heard Papa." Julia came up behind her and looked at Papa. "Do you want to tell us now or wait until after supper?"

"I might as well tell you now," he said as he handed her the letter. "I've found you a husband."

"You what?" Julia widened her eyes. "I don't think I heard correctly."

"You heard me just fine, Julia. Remember how Nelda Montague filled out that application to be a mail order bride last year?"

Julia sank back on her heels and nodded. "Yes, and she headed out west, all by herself, to marry some man she'd never even met."

"Well ..." Papa's expression turned more solemn as he held Julia's gaze. "Her folks say she's happy, so I figured it just might work out for you."

"No." She shook her head. "I will not be a mail order bride."

Papa's jaw tightened. "I'm not exactly giving you a choice. Open that envelope and see what's inside."

Her hands shook as she slipped her fingers inside the envelope and pulled out the contents—a handwritten note and a train ticket. Her heart sank. Papa was more serious than she'd seen him since Mama's funeral.

"I really don't—"

He shook his head as he backed away from his daughters. "This is something we have to do. You have to understand that I'm not getting any younger, and it's getting more and more difficult for me to feed you and—"

"I can get a job ... like Mary did."

"In case you haven't noticed, there are no jobs in town ... at least not for decent, God-loving young women. Mary got the only one out there, and it's not even secure."

"But Papa—"

"The deal has already been made. You will be leaving in exactly one week. The man's name is Stone Michaels, and he has already made arrangements for you to stay with the pastor of his church until you are married."

Julia turned to look at her sister who'd remained unusually silent since Papa told them about the contents of the envelope. Sarah's eyes were still open wide, and her face was pale.

"Come on, Sarah. Let's finish getting supper ready."

Papa turned and headed for his bedroom. "Call me when it's ready. I need to get a load off these tired feet."

As soon as he left, Sarah grabbed Julia by the arm and spun her around. "We can't let him do this to you."

Julia let out a sardonic snicker. "What choice do I have? Papa is right. There are no jobs in town for a woman like me."

"But—" Sarah hung her head before raising it again to look directly at Julia. "Whatever will I do without you here?"

"Everything I do." Julia sighed and forced a smile. "It won't be so bad. At least you'll have Lenora nearby if you need anything. And I'm sure Mary will be able to talk to you if there's an emergency."

A tear trickled down Sarah's cheek. "I will miss you so much."

Julia felt the backs of her eyes stinging as well, but she'd trained herself not to cry. She needed to stay strong.

The week went by quickly, and Julia's hope for Papa to change his mind didn't come to be. Every now and then she saw a look of concern on his face, but when he saw her staring at him, he looked away.

She loaded up her belongings onto the carriage for Papa to take her to the train station. Sarah wanted to go, but Papa instructed her to stay behind so she could start supper for him. The look she gave Julia would have been funny if Julia hadn't been so torn up inside about where she was going.

"What if he's not there when I arrive?" she asked Papa.

"He will be. I have communicated with his pastor who has assured me that Stone Michaels is a good man who loves the Lord ... and he honors his word."

"I don't see why he had to send off for someone he doesn't even know."

"Stop this right now, Julia. You're only making it more difficult for yourself."

From the look on his face, she could tell it wasn't easy for him either. He must have felt desperate to go to such measures.

All the way to the station, Julia thought about how difficult things had become. As it was, they were already relying on the goodwill from some of the people from church in order to put food on the table. Papa's pride had taken a big hit when one of the ladies handed him a basket filled with enough food to last a week.

Now that she thought about it, moving away was probably the best thing for the family. Even though she still didn't want to, she was willing to sacrifice so Papa could rest a little bit more. It might even be good for Sarah to gain some maturity. As long as Julia was around, there was no reason for her to grow up.

Papa backed away as it came time for her to board the train. But as soon as she took the first step, he came running up to her. "Stop. I don't want you to go. I have changed my mind."

Julia looked down at Papa whose red eyes belied his earlier determination to marry her off. "No, you were right, Papa. I have to go."

The pain deepened the lines on his face. "But we can figure something out."

She forced a smile and shook her head. "If you had said

this earlier, I would have stayed, but now that I'm here, I think this is the best thing ... for all of us."

His chin quivered as he reached up and touched her hand. "I love you, Julia. I never want you to forget that. If I didn't have to—"

The conductor interrupted him, calling out that everyone needed to clear the way to close the door. Once seated, she looked out the window and saw her father standing by the track, tears streaming down his cheeks. The fear of what she was about to face was replaced by pity for Papa who didn't know what else to do.

*

Stone stood by the railroad track, watching for the train. He pulled out his handkerchief and wiped his forehead before putting it back in his pocket. In spite of the fact that he'd made this decision on his own, he now wondered if it had been a good one.

Pastor Ledbetter had offered to pick up Stone's intended bride, but he felt that it was his duty. In fact, it was his responsibility to make sure she was well taken care of from the moment she stepped off the train until ... well, until one of them died. He shuddered. This decision was one that would be with him for the rest of his life.

The rumbling vibration signaled that the train was just around the corner. Stone fixed his eyes on the engine as soon as it appeared, and his heart thumped harder the closer it got.

When it finally came to a stop and let off a final puff of steam, he said a silent prayer for guidance before stepping closer to the train. He opened his eyes and stared back at the train, his gaze settling on the door that the conductor had opened.

Several people disembarked before he finally saw her. He was amazed by how much prettier she looked than the picture her father had sent. He'd expected someone less attractive and meeker. Instead, he saw a girl with chestnut colored hair, large dark brown eyes, and a softness that her

9

photograph didn't convey.

She stood at the top step as she surveyed the crowd below. The instant they made eye contact, he was aware that she knew who he was. Her features tightened, and her face looked pinched just like in the picture.

At first, he couldn't move. He just stood there staring at her, willing her to relax so he could see the pretty girl who'd stepped off the train. But instead, the longer she looked at him the more puckered she appeared.

Chapter 2

(Golden, Colorado)

"Julia?" he said softly.

"You must be Mr. Michaels."

"Stone." He extended a hand to help her down.

She lifted an eyebrow as she held his gaze momentarily. And then she lifted her chin. "I prefer to call you Mr. Michaels."

He let out a deep sigh. "Whatever makes you happy. Do you mind if I call you Julia?"

One corner of her mouth tipped up. "You may call me whatever you like. You have purchased me fair and square."

Stone frowned. This wasn't at all what he'd hoped for. She far surpassed what he expected in the looks department, even when she wasn't smiling, but her surly attitude left him wishing he'd accepted the younger daughter that their father had initially told him about.

"Please, Julia ... Miss Hollister. I didn't intend—" Oh, what was the use? He could now see that she didn't want to be here, and she had clearly worked herself up over coming against her will that she had him pegged as the enemy.

She took a look around. "Colorado is quite different from Virginia."

"Yes, I know. How was your train ride?"

"Very long and tiring."

"Then why don't we head on over to the pastor's house where you will be staying? They're expecting you soon anyway."

She nodded but didn't say another word until they got in the carriage. She ran her fingers over the edge of the seat. "This is quite nice. You must be very successful at whatever it is you do."

"Didn't your father tell you?" He picked up the reins and guided his horse toward the road leading to the pastor's house.

"He told me you do some sort of farming and that you live in the mountains."

Stone chuckled. "I am a cattle rancher, and yes, I do live at the foot of the mountains. Like you, I'm originally from the East, but when people started heading west, my adventurous nature pulled me here." He didn't need to tell her about his parents and brothers dying in a house fire—at least not yet.

"But you forgot one thing."

He turned to her. "What is that?"

"You forgot to find a woman to bring with you."

He grimaced. "I didn't exactly forget. It just didn't cross my mind that there wouldn't be any women here ... at least not any single ones."

"Come on, Mr. Michaels. There must be some single women."

"If there are, I haven't met any." He paused to gather his thoughts about what to tell her next. She clearly didn't realize just how successful he'd become, and he wasn't sure if he should tell her. So he decided to talk around that topic. "After I sold some of the land I'd purchased from another business venture, I was able to build a house." He smiled at her before turning back to the dusty road. "I made sure it was a nice one and plenty big for a houseful of children."

"That was mighty presumptuous of you," she said.

"Maybe so, but I do want a big family some day." He smiled at her, hoping to get one in return. To his surprise, a flicker of a smile tweaked her lips, but it ended quickly. "I would like to share all of my blessings with a wife and children."

"Well, it appears that you've found the wife. Now all you have to do is find yourself some children."

This woman was a feisty one. He steered the horse around the final bend, until they spotted the pastor's house in a clearing. It was a small white ranch-style home that was separated from the church by an expansive field of clover.

"At least the pastor has a nice home." She cleared her throat. "It is much nicer than the one I left."

Stone wondered what she'd think of his house that was more than double the size of this one. "This is a very comfortable house, and I am sure you will enjoy your stay."

*

They hadn't come to a complete stop when a middle-aged couple who appeared slightly younger than Papa stepped out onto the front porch, grins on both of their faces. The man appeared to be of average height, while his wife barely came up to his chin. Both of them had pleasant expressions on their faces.

The woman approached the carriage first, her smile widening as she got closer. "It is so good to see you, Stone." She turned to Julia and held open her arms. "You must be Julia. I am delighted that you will be staying in our home." She gave Julia a warm embrace that reminded her of Mama's hugs.

"I am ... um ... pleased to be here." Julia had no idea how to respond, but she didn't want to appear entirely ungrateful. The train ride gave her a chance to think about how much she didn't want to come. "This is all so different from what I'm used to."

"Oh, I know, dear. Edwin—that's my husband the pastor—well, he and I came here from New York where he pastored a church in the upper part of the state. When the call came that he was needed here, we had to spend a lot of time in prayer before we gave our answer."

The pastor extended his hand. "I am Pastor Ledbetter. Welcome to Colorado."

She took his hand. "Thank you, Pastor."

"Why don't we show you to your room?" He gestured toward the house. "Martha, you lead the way."

The instant Julia walked inside the house, it was evident that these people were better off than Papa. The house appeared even larger once she got inside, and the furnishings were much more lavish than any she'd seen back in Virginia.

"This is lovely," she said softly.

"If you like this, just wait until you see your house." Martha smiled. "Or has Stone not told you about it yet?" She turned to Stone. "You should have at least sent her some pictures."

"She will see it in due time," Stone said. "I need to be getting on back to the ranch before it gets dark."

"I prepared some food for you to take back with you." Martha turned to Julia. "Why don't you come to the kitchen with me and help me get it ready?"

Julia was amazed by how large and nice the kitchen was. "I would love to be able to cook here. I hope you allow me to while I am staying with you."

Martha stopped, took Julia's hands in hers, and squeezed. "Dear girl, you have no idea how well you will be taken care of once you marry Stone. His kitchen is so much nicer. In fact, his house is so large it makes this one look like a shack." She gave Julia a warm smile. "But if you want to cook while you are here, then by all means, I would love for you to. It will give me a break, and I'm sure you have some recipes that I have never tried."

"My cooking is rather simple," Julia said. "But my father and sisters seem to enjoy it."

"I'm sure I will too." Martha pointed to a stack of baskets by the pantry. "Can you hand me a couple of those baskets please?"

The two of them spent the next several minutes filling the baskets with ham, biscuits, and jars of jam, all wrapped in gingham napkins. "This should be enough to last him a couple of days."

Stone's eyes lit up at the sight of the food baskets. "You shouldn't have gone to all this trouble, Mrs. Ledbetter."

"How many times do I have to tell you to call me Martha?" She nodded toward the door. "Let's get this in your carriage. I don't want your cattle to starve to death, so you'd better be getting on home soon."

Once they had the carriage loaded up with food, Stone asked if he could speak to Julia in private. "Yes, of course," the pastor said as he turned to his wife. "Let's go inside and leave these two to talk."

"Julia, it is painfully obvious that you came against your will." Stone clamped his mouth shut and swallowed hard. She could sense that he was as distressed as she was. "If you decide you want to return to Virginia, I will buy your ticket and send you back. But I would like for you to at least give Colorado … and me a chance."

She blinked as she sensed the sincerity in his voice. She finally gave him a clipped nod. "That is fair enough."

"That's all I ask." He started to turn toward his horse and carriage but stopped and faced her again. "When would you like to see my ranch?"

She held her hands out. "Whenever you want me to."

"Would tomorrow be too soon?" The expectant look on his face softened her heart.

"Tomorrow will be just fine."

He tipped his hat. "I'll be here in the morning to take you there." Then he got in his carriage and left.

Julia stood on the porch and watched as he disappeared around the cluster of trees on the edge of the property. When she turned around, she saw Martha looking at her.

"Stone is a sweet and godly young man. I think you will be very happy with him," Martha said. "Come on inside, and I'll show you to your room. My husband has already brought your suitcase in there."

The guest room was much more lavishly decorated than any Julia had ever seen. "This is lovely."

Martha smiled. "I hope you are comfortable here. Come on out when you are ready to eat, and we can have what is left of what I cooked for Stone."

Julia was still a little bit nervous, but she relaxed some during dinner. Pastor Ledbetter and Martha did everything in their power to make her feel at home. Martha even drew her a warm bath. After days and days of riding on the train, she was happy to soak away some of the dirt. She went to bed feeling fresh and clean but tired.

It took her a while to fall asleep. Her thoughts drifted back to the image of Papa's face as the train pulled away. Before they'd left her home in Virginia, she would have gladly stayed, but once they were at the station, she knew her father had run out of options, or they wouldn't have been there. There was no doubt in her mind that he loved her and he would miss her.

During the long ride from Virginia to Colorado, she had time to think about her life, and she'd decided to go back home as soon as it was feasible. Marrying for anything but love wasn't something she wanted for herself. She would much rather be without a husband than have a farce of a marriage. Since Papa couldn't support her, she decided to take in people's mending to add to the family's coffers. Surely Papa wouldn't object to that. With this in mind, she was able to relax and fall asleep.

The next morning, she awoke to the sound of Stone's voice. She sat up in bed and took a long look around the room, letting the situation sink in a little deeper. Her initial fear returned, but she took a couple of deep breaths that helped. She got up and started getting ready for the day. Fifteen minutes later, she walked out into the main living area of the house.

Stone's face lit up when he saw her, but his smile quickly faded. "Are you ready to see the ranch?"

She nodded. "I suppose."

He told Martha that he would have her back by dark. On their way to the carriage, he spoke softly. "Remember what I told you yesterday—that if you don't want to stay, I can send you back."

"Yes, I remember."

"If you decide to stay, I will change anything in the house that you want changed. As it is now, the decorations leave quite a bit to be desired."

Julia forced a smile. She wondered if Stone was always this polite or if he was just pretending to be for her sake. Whatever the case, she needed to stay on guard.

The moment he stopped in front of a large iron gate with his last name emblazoned on an overhead arch, she gasped. What Martha had said about his ranch was an understatement. The house that was barely visible off in the distance looked like a mansion. Not only was it the biggest house she'd ever seen, it was made of stone—something she was sure must have cost a fortune.

Chapter 3

"This is my home," Stone said. "And it will be yours as well if you decide to stay." He got out of the carriage, opened the gate, guided the horse and carriage to the other side, closed the gate, and gestured around. "I have several hundred acres. I had more a few years ago, but I sold some of it off because I didn't need it."

Julia had never seen anything like this. "Did you, by any chance, send my father a picture of this?"

He shook his head. "No. Why?"

"I don't think he would have let me come if you had."

Stone shot her a quizzical look. "Why not?"

"He would have thought you were lying."

"Lying?" He cocked his head to the side, giving her puzzled look. "Why would he think such a thing?"

"It is just so ..." She waved her hands around. "So big and ... well, unreal."

He laughed. "Oh, it's very real." He held out his calloused hands. "I feel the realness of it all every evening after I finish my work."

"Are you ..." She hesitated but only for a moment. "Are you rich?"

Stone shoved his hands in his pockets and sighed. "I suppose you could say I have quite a bit of money, but I don't believe that's what makes a person rich."

Julia blinked. If she were anyone else, she might be so impressed that she could overlook the fact that she barely knew this man. But she wasn't that easily swayed by things. She still didn't know him well enough to commit her life to him.

"Would you like to see inside?" he asked.

"Yes, of course."

He steered the horse to the front of the house, got out of the carriage, and helped her out. "I haven't had the time to plant any flowers yet. If you decide you want to stay, you can choose what you want."

She tightened her jaw. She didn't want him to think that she was only interested in his wealth, but she had to admit, if only to herself, she was even more impressed with the house up close.

"Let's go inside." He walked up the steps and opened the front door.

As she walked inside, she saw a large fireplace with a stately mantle that held a row of framed photographs. She pointed. "Who are those people?"

His expression turned guarded as he pointed. "These are my parents, and the other ones are my brothers."

"Are they here in Colorado?"

He shook his head. "No, unfortunately, they all passed away before I came here."

Julia gasped. "All of them?"

He nodded. "Yes, there was a house fire, and none of them could get out in time before they perished."

"I am so sorry." Her hand went to her mouth. She couldn't imagine living through anything so horrific.

"That's why I chose to build my house with stone."

Since she wasn't planning to stick around, she figured she might as well ask questions. "That must have cost you a fortune."

He held her gaze before slowly nodding. "I suppose you would like to know how I came into money."

She shrugged. "That thought did cross my mind."

"Let me show you around, and then we'll go into the kitchen and talk."

As they walked through the house, she continued to be more impressed with each room. In addition to the main living area, there was a smaller space for more intimate conversation. He walked past what he called the library, even though it only had one small row of books. Upstairs, there were five bedrooms. Not only did the house have more rooms than she expected, every single one of them had a fireplace.

"Let's go down to the kitchen now."

She followed him back downstairs, wondering if she'd ever figure out her way around this place. As they reached the kitchen, she gasped again. Every conceivable convenience was in this room.

"Do you cook?" she asked.

He shook his head. "No, but I thought it would be a good idea to have a well appointed kitchen for when God blessed me with a woman to share my life with." He gestured toward one of the chairs around the table. "Have a seat. I'll put on a kettle for some tea." He paused. "Or do you prefer coffee?"

"No, tea is fine." Julia could picture herself cooking in this beautiful kitchen. As Stone prepared the tea, she closed her eyes, and the first thing that popped into her head was the image of a child coming toward her while she stood in front of the stove. Her eyes popped open.

"What are you thinking about?" he asked.

She shook her head. "Nothing important."

A few minutes later they sat adjacent to each other at the table. An overwhelming sense of peace flowed through her, but she quickly shook it off. She had no business feeling this way since she'd soon be on a train heading back to Virginia.

"So I suppose I should tell you how all of this came to be."

She sat and listened as he explained how he'd been away when his parents' house had burned to the ground. He was the oldest boy, and his brothers were still in their teens.

"My father had lost his job, so I went to work on the railroad to send money home." He gave her a weak smile. "It has been almost seven years, but when I talk about it, I feel as though it was last week."

"I understand if you can't continue."

"No, this is something you need to know."

She lifted her chin in a brief nod. As she studied his face, she saw something she hadn't noticed before—a look of calm determination.

After the fire, he couldn't stand the thought of remaining in New York, so he headed west for the adventure and to get away from the pain. His first stop was the mountains near Golden, Colorado, where gold miners were striking it rich. He worked hard, until he had enough money to buy some land and cattle.

"Back then, land was very cheap, so I purchased much more than I would ever need," he explained. "After holding onto it for a few years, the value increased so much that I was able to sell it and make a nice profit."

"And that is how you were able to build this house?"

He nodded. "I continued working in the gold mines for some time, but after a while, I decided it was time to settle down and focus on building my ranch."

She was impressed that everything he owned had come from hard work and determination. "I have to admit, I didn't expect all of this."

"Does it sway your decision?" His gaze locked with hers, and she sensed that the way she answered was more important to him than what her answer was.

Chapter 4

"I'm sorry, Mr. Michaels, but all the money in the world cannot affect my decision. I am still not sure I can stay."

"Then why did you come?" he asked. "I know your father made a promise, but I would have understood if you'd decided you couldn't do it."

She fidgeted with the handle of her cup before meeting his gaze again. "It was important to Papa. He has struggled so much keeping food on the table. I offered to get a job, but he reminded me that jobs are hard to come by for anyone, especially single women."

"What will you do when ... if you go back?"

His question was so matter-of-fact, she was taken aback. "I-I'm not sure. Maybe take in some mending or other small tasks."

"If you still want to return after a week, as I already mentioned, I will buy your train ticket to Virginia." He swallowed hard. "And I can send some money to help your family."

She blinked as her eyebrows shot up. "You would do that?"

He nodded. "Yes, absolutely. I don't like seeing

hardworking people struggle." He gave her a half-smile. "And I believe that is what the Lord would want me to do."

Julia had to stifle the urge to jump out of her chair, throw her arms around his neck, and give him a huge hug. But she didn't do that. She forced herself to remain sitting like a lady, holding back her emotions while tears nearly exploded from her eyes.

*

Stone was amazed by the way Julia maintained her dignity, although she was clearly impressed with her surroundings. He'd worked hard for it, but he didn't think it was as big of a deal as some others did. Julia's reactions let him know that his wealth wasn't enough to keep her in Golden, and in spite of the fact that he needed a wife he liked that about her.

While someone else might have been put off by the way she acted, he found her more attractive as he got to know her. He wanted to beg her to give him a chance, but doing so might prolong something that wasn't meant to be. So he closed his eyes and prayed for the Lord to bless him with what he needed rather than what he wanted.

When he opened his eyes, he saw her staring at him. He smiled.

"Do you pray a lot?"

He nodded. "I do."

"So do I."

He stood up to get more tea. "If it weren't for the Lord and His mercies, I don't know how I would have gotten through the difficult times after I lost my family."

"Same with my family. After Mama died, Papa was so depressed he couldn't do anything besides get up and go to work. My older sister Lenora didn't waste much time marrying after Mama passed away, so I was left with all of the household duties."

"How old were you?"

She looked into his eyes and saw genuine interest, so she continued. "Barely fourteen."

"That must have been difficult." He tried to imagine a much younger version of this woman, cooking and cleaning for a family.

"It was, but now that I look back, I see that it was only because I didn't know what I was doing. Mama shouldered quite a bit of responsibility, and I had to take over."

"Is Sarah going to take over for you ... at least until you return?"

Her eyes crinkled with amusement. "I wish I could say yes, but Sarah is ... well, she still has the spirit of a child."

"Does she have something wrong with her?"

Julia shook her head. "No, there is absolutely nothing wrong with that girl, other than a playfulness that starts when she wakes up every morning and doesn't end until she goes to bed at night."

"So I heard."

"I think most men would find her attractive ... that is, if they don't mind cooking their own meals and cleaning up after her." She gave him one of her rare grins that melted his heart.

He laughed. "Beauty goes much deeper than the face."

"She's very sweet. In fact, of all of the sisters, she is probably the nicest one."

"It's easy to be nice when you don't have much responsibility," he said.

She narrowed her gaze, tilted her head, and gave him an odd look. "Yes, I think you're right. But Sarah gets along with everyone." She smiled again. "And by everyone, I'm including adults, children, and animals."

"Then she might like living on a ranch."

"She would, but I doubt she'd do much work. She'd be too busy playing with the animals."

"Maybe if ..." He tightened his lips as he tried to decide whether or not to continue. Oh well, what would it hurt to say what was on his mind? "Perhaps if you change your mind in the next week and decide to stay here in Colorado, we could have her come and visit. She'd have plenty of livestock to play with, and she would make you feel less homesick."

He'd half hoped for a response to let him know she might consider it, but instead, her smile faded a bit as she dropped her gaze to the table. He still didn't regret saying it, though. It would give her something else to think about.

"Would you like for me to cook some supper before you take me back to the pastor's house?"

He sank back in his chair, folding his arms. The thought of a home-cooked meal that wasn't left over from yesterday appealed to him, but he didn't want to take advantage of someone who didn't want to be here in the first place.

"I really don't mind," she said softly. "In fact, I would love to cook a meal in this kitchen." She looked around. "I have never seen such a beautiful stove in my life."

"Do you want to know a secret?" he asked.

She gave him a curious look. "Secret?"

He nodded. "If you cook for me, you will be the first to ever use that stove."

She hopped up from the chair. "Then wild horses won't be able to stop me. Not only have I never seen such a beautiful stove, I have never been the first person to use one."

"Before you cook, why don't we go out to the small garden I have behind the house? It is too early for anything to be ready yet, but I would like to show you what I have planted." When he saw the look of concern on her face, he pointed to the pantry. "I have plenty of vegetables in the pantry. Some of the ladies from church canned last year's harvest and brought me enough jars to last through the winter."

"Do you have any meat?"

He smiled and nodded. "There is some cured ham in the pantry."

"I'm surprised you have ham with all those cows out

there."

"One of the neighboring ranches also has pigs and chickens. If you like fresh eggs, I'll be happy to buy you some chickens."

He led the way out the back door. The back was even more breathtaking than the front. He made a sweeping gesture over the land. "I own all of the land as far as you can see in that direction and on the other side to the foot of the mountains."

"That is a lot of land."

"I had three times as much land until I sold some of it off. A man only needs so much."

When they returned to the kitchen, he placed his basket on the counter. "Do you need some help in here?"

She shook her head. "Just show me how to turn this thing on, and I can get right to work."

Once she had the stove fired up, he left to feed the cows. Something about having a woman in the house made it feel more like a home.

He did his work as quickly as possible, turning around and looking at the house every so often. The mental image of how he'd left her standing at the stove in the apron she'd found on a peg in the pantry made him smile.

After he had everything done, he headed back to the house. As soon as he opened the door, the aroma of fresh food cooking grabbed his senses and pulled him back to the kitchen.

She glanced over her shoulder and grinned. "Cooking on this stove is so much fun."

"So you enjoy cooking, do you?"

"I've always enjoyed it," she said, "but I have to admit it gets tiring to constantly have to prepare the exact same meal, day in and day out."

"Maybe we can catch some fish for another night," he said tentatively, hoping it wouldn't frighten her. "The river is packed with trout."

She stilled, holding the spoon over the pot. "I haven't had fish in ages. Papa says they're too expensive."

"That's because he doesn't live next to a river. We can just go catch whatever we need when we want to ... and we don't have to pay a dime."

*

Julia felt an internal fight between loving this kitchen, the house, and the thought of being able to eat whatever she wanted when she wanted, and being frustrated about Papa sending her off to marry someone she didn't know. For all Papa knew, Stone could have been a horrible man.

She had to admit he was someone she would have been attracted to if she'd met him on her own. But the fact remained, he'd sent off for a wife—any wife—so she couldn't pretend that he was so madly in love he wanted to marry her for who she was. It was strictly an arranged marriage ... a marriage of convenience ... his convenience.

It pleased Julia to see Stone eat so eagerly, going back for seconds and thirds. "I'm glad you're enjoying the meal."

He put down his fork, placed his forearms on the table, and leaned toward her. "You are a wonderful cook. Your father never told me that."

"For that matter, he never told me that either."

"Perhaps he didn't have anything to compare it to."

Julia shook her head. "Mama was a wonderful cook, and fortunately, I was able to learn from her before she got sick and passed away."

"Do your sisters cook?"

"Mary can cook, which is why the wealthy family in town hired her to look after their children. Lenora cooks, but she doesn't really like it. When she got married, there were days when I went to her house and helped her put the meal on the table before her husband got home." She glanced down at the table as the memory of what happened returned.

"What's wrong, Julia?"

She looked back up at Stone who looked at her with

27

sincere concern in his eyes. "Her husband was a banker, and he was killed in a bank holdup."

"I am terribly sorry."

"Her husband left her with some money, but I'm afraid she might be running out. It's difficult for her to be on her own with a small child."

Stone chewed his bottom lip as they held a gaze for a long moment. She could tell he was deep in thought.

Chapter 5

Stone realized that Julia had been through her own share of difficulties. He'd once been bitter because he thought no one else would understand what he'd been through, but he suspected she had some idea based on her own personal experiences.

"I would like to help your whole family," he said. "I know you said you don't want to marry me, but there must be a reason God brought you here. Maybe He wanted me to use my blessings to bless your family."

The look on Julia's face was haunting. "That won't be necessary," she said as she pushed away from the table. "The train ticket will be plenty. Can you take me to the pastor's house after I finish cleaning the kitchen?"

He nodded. "I'll help you."

"I can do it by myself," she said as she started clearing the table. "I'm used to it."

He took hold of her wrist. She stilled and met his gaze with the same haunted look. "Julia, I want to help. You don't have to do everything all by yourself when you are here."

She blinked and then nodded. "Fine. I can wash the dishes."

"And I will dry them." He let go of her wrist but maintained eye contact until she looked away.

They cleaned the kitchen in silence, but he enjoyed having her with him. He never went without food, even when he was alone, but his normal routine was lonely and miserable in spite of the fine surroundings. Even though she didn't love him—and it didn't appear she'd stick around long enough to let it happen—he already knew he liked her. A lot. And he suspected he could fall in love with her in due time. But one thing he couldn't do was to make her love him back.

"We need to get going before it starts getting dark," he said as he hung the towel on the rack.

"I wish you didn't have to take me back so late."

He wished the same thing, only for a different reason. But there was no point in bringing it up … at least not now. Maybe never. She didn't appear to be budging in the least with her resolve to return to Virginia.

"Let's go." He picked up her coat and helped her into it. "At least it isn't as cold as it will be soon."

They made small talk all the way to the pastor's house. "I can get out on my own," she said.

He started to argue but decided against it. There was no point in saying anything. He waited until she went inside before turning around and heading back to his ranch.

*

"How did it go, dear?" Martha asked as soon as Julia walked into the living room.

"Very nicely. He has a lovely home, and he let me cook on his stove. Did you know that it was never used until today?"

Martha chuckled. "I'm not surprised. Most of the women in the church send him home with food, so he doesn't really need to use it."

Julia tilted her head. "You say most women. Why hasn't he been able to find a wife here?"

"Because all of the women at the church have husbands.

Believe me when I tell you that we would welcome single women with open arms." Martha pointed to the chair beside her. "Have a seat so I don't feel like you might take off at any moment."

Julia sat in the chair. "I would think that there would be some ... like perhaps a sister or daughter who came along for the adventure."

"That would be nice. I can't say that has never happened, but as soon as a young woman appears, some eligible bachelor snaps her right up."

"You make it sound like we're a commodity."

Martha shook her head. "Not exactly a commodity. More of an oddity. That is why so many of the men are looking in the catalogs or finding ways to meet women through the mail."

"Catalogs?" Julia narrowed her eyes. "Women are listed in catalogs?"

"They are, complete with information such as their age, whether or not they can cook, if they like children or music ..." She lifted her hands and let them drop in her lap. "They include anything that gives enough information for the men to choose one for his wife."

Then a horrible thought crossed Julia's mind. "Was I in a catalog?"

"No, dear. Your father found an advertisement that Stone sent through the church. You see, it was imperative to him to find a Christian woman with good morals and values."

That made Julia feel a little bit better. "What else do you know about how my father started communicating with Stone?"

"Just that he said his daughters loved the Lord and that he wanted to make sure they had good homes with men who could love them."

That didn't sound terrible, but Julia would have preferred to find her own husband. The problem was that she never went anywhere.

Martha covered Julia's hands with her own. "Why don't we pray about this?"

Julia nodded. "That would be nice."

After Martha prayed, she thought about what she would want in a husband. As far as she could tell, Stone had exactly what she wanted—and then some. She never imagined herself living in such a fine house as what he had, and his gentlemanly ways appeared deeply ingrained.

"What are you thinking, dear?" Martha asked after several minutes of silence.

Julia closed her eyes again and shook her head. "I am so confused."

"Perhaps you can talk about it now, and I can help you sort through your confusing thoughts."

Julia smiled as she opened her eyes and looked Martha in the eyes. Although this woman looked nothing like Mama, she had the same gentle mannerisms and ability to comfort her.

"My mother loved roses."

Instead of questioning Julia's comment that had nothing to do with what they had been discussing, she offered a comforting smile. "Roses are lovely, aren't they?"

"Yes. In fact, one of my favorite things to do each day after my chores inside are done is to go outside and tend to a white rose bush we planted not long before she passed away."

Martha gently squeezed Julia's hand. "It's nice that you have something to remember her by."

"Except I am here and the roses are back in Virginia."

"You left a lot of yourself back in Virginia." Martha let go of Julia's hand and leaned back in her chair. "I can't say I fully understand what you are going through because when I came here, Edwin and I were already married. But I did leave family and friends and a house I loved when Edwin was asked to come to Colorado."

Julia cleared her throat. "Do you ever wish you hadn't

come here?"

"In the beginning, perhaps, but this is my home now. I love the friends I have made here. In fact, they have become like family to me."

Julia thought back to her life in Virginia. She had her family, her home, and her church, but outside of that, she had nothing. Papa relied on her to do the household chores. Sarah looked at her as a way of avoiding hard work because she knew Julia would do it for her. Mary rarely came around. Occasionally, Lenora asked for her help, but she was so busy with her child she had little time for anything else.

After Mama passed away, some of the church members brought meals, but then they all eventually got back to their own lives and seemed to have forgotten about her. The only time she saw most of them was on Sunday mornings, and even then, they gave her pitying looks as they avoided her and her family. Looking around here, she saw that Martha was surrounded by blessings—from a husband who clearly adored her to a church that sounded like one filled with people who cared about each other.

"Do you think you might reconsider and stay here in Colorado?" Martha asked.

Julia blinked back a tear that had formed and shrugged. "I don't know. This is a very difficult decision."

"I know it is, dear. But you do realize you don't have to make a decision right away, don't you?" Martha paused. "I have known Stone for several years now, and I know that he is a patient man who wouldn't want you to do anything you don't want to do."

In the short time Julia had known Stone, there was no doubt in her mind that Martha was describing him with truth. "I know."

"And you are welcome to stay here until you make your decision."

Julia sighed and smiled. "Thank you."

"You look exhausted. Why don't you go to your room and

get some rest? When you get up in the morning, you can eat a hearty breakfast before we run a few errands."

"Errands?"

Martha nodded. "I have to take some food to a few people who haven't been feeling well, and then we can visit one of the members who just had a baby."

That sounded like fun to Julia. "How about Mr. Michaels? Do you think we should stop by his ranch to cook him some supper?"

Martha tilted her head and gave her a curious look. "Did you tell him you would do that?"

"No, but I—" Julia stopped because she wasn't sure why she thought she might be expected to do that.

"I suspect you probably feel that you owe Stone something, but you don't. And he doesn't expect anything from you."

Julia cast her gaze downward. Martha had gotten it right. She did feel that she owed Stone something, and all she had to give at the moment was her cooking ability.

"But if you want to do that, I'm sure he wouldn't mind," Martha said.

Julia went to bed and slept quite well. She awoke to the aroma of breakfast cooking. It seemed odd to have someone else prepare her meals since she'd been the one to do it over the years since Mama had passed.

Martha pointed to the coffee. "Pour yourself a cup. I'll have breakfast on the table in two shakes of a donkey's tail."

The bacon, eggs and biscuits were delicious, but Julia was happy to help clean up so they could run their errands. She helped Martha pack some baskets of food for the sick people and another basket filled with items for the new baby.

Everyone was happy to see them, but they didn't spend much time with the families of the sick people. They brought the food, prayed with the families, chatted for just a few minutes, and moved on.

"I've discovered that it's best not to overstay, even though they seem to enjoy having someone stop by," Martha explained. "Maybe we can go back in a few days." She grinned. "Are you ready to go see the new baby?"

Julia nodded. "I've always enjoyed babies."

Martha gave her a knowing look but didn't say anything. They rode to the next house in silence.

Once they got to the door of the house, they heard the sound of the baby's wailing. "I hope everything is okay."

A harried older woman answered the door, her face tight with worry. "We can't figure out what is wrong with little Richard. He won't stop crying."

"Do you think he might be sick?" Martha asked.

"I don't think so. He isn't running a fever."

Julia stepped forward. "May I hold him?"

The woman looked at Martha who nodded. "Yes, I suppose you may, but you will probably want to put him down. That boy has some loud lungs."

Martha pointed toward the room where the sound was coming from. "Is he in there?"

"Yes, he is in there with my daughter. We have tried everything from walking with him to rocking him, but nothing has worked."

"Let's see what we can do." Martha knocked lightly on the door and opened it when a woman's voice invited them in. "Hi, Elizabeth. We just stopped by to bring you a few things for you and your baby. This is my friend Julia from Virginia."

The young woman sitting in the rocking chair holding the crying baby gave her a brief glance, but she was clearly so upset and flustered about the baby crying that she didn't say anything. Martha nudged her forward.

"May I?" Julia said as she held out her hands.

Without a moment's hesitation, she thrust the baby toward her. Julia pulled little Richard close to her chest, and he instantly stopped crying.

Elizabeth chin dropped. "That is the first time he has

stopped crying all day."

Julia shook her head before looking down into the baby's eyes. "I think sometimes they just need someone different to look at."

Martha stepped closer and pushed back the blanket to get a better look at Richard. "He looks very sweet."

His little face scrunched up, and he puckered his lip. Julia changed his position. "I think he might have gas."

Over the next several minutes, she managed to get a few burps out of him. By the time they left, he'd fallen asleep.

"We must go now." Martha walked toward the door and stopped. "Maybe I can come by again in a few days."

"Please come sooner," Elizabeth said as she turned to Julia. "And you are welcome to come too. Thank you so much for helping me with the baby. I was at my wit's end."

As Julia and Martha pulled away in the carriage, Martha chuckled. "You are excellent with babies. You need some of your own."

"That was what Mama used to say, but without a husband—"

Martha glanced at her before turning back to the road. Julia was glad she didn't say anything.

When they arrived at the ranch, they saw that the gate was open, so they didn't have to get out of the carriage. Julia spotted Stone standing on the front porch as they drew closer.

"Did he know we were coming?" Julia asked.

"I didn't tell him."

Chapter 6

Stone thought he might see Julia today, but until now he wasn't sure. All he could do was hope. He'd finished his chores early, just in case, and now he was glad he did.

He stepped off the porch to help Julia and Martha out of the carriage. "It is good to see you ladies. Would you like to come in?"

Martha smiled at Julia who spoke. "We came so I could cook you some supper."

"You didn't have to do that." His stomach rumbled, belying his words. "But I certainly do appreciate it."

Martha laughed. "I would imagine you do. Why don't you go on inside and start Stone's supper while I chat with him out here?"

Julia glanced at Stone, and as soon as he nodded, she did what Martha had asked. Once she went inside, Stone turned to the pastor's wife. "What did you want to talk to me about?"

"Why don't we walk around to your garden while we talk?"

"Okay." He followed her as she went around behind the house.

She pointed to the small section where he grew vegetables. "What all do you plan to grow?"

He shoved his hands in his pockets and looked toward the garden he'd already started. "Beans, corn, tomatoes, potatoes, squash, and whatever else I can get."

"How about some roses?"

"Roses?" He looked at Martha. "Why roses?"

"Well ... I just happen to know that Julia loves white roses." She told him about the rose bush Julia had mentioned. "It brings back fond memories of the times she spent with her mother."

At that moment, Stone new exactly what he needed to do. "I'll think about it."

"Good boy. Now let's get on in the house and see if we can give Julia a hand."

By the time they entered the kitchen, Julia had a couple of pots and a skillet on the stove. She smiled at him. "I made a cobbler with the peaches I found in the pantry, and it's in the oven."

Every time Stone looked at Julia she got prettier and prettier, and he felt an overwhelming sense of satisfaction, knowing he'd have a delicious meal soon. The only thing that could make him happier was if she would agree to stay and become his wife. But he still wasn't about to push her into anything she didn't want, just because it would make him feel more complete.

After she pulled the cobbler out of the oven, she turned to him. "Everything is ready for you to eat. I tried not to dirty up too many pots so you wouldn't have much to clean later."

"We'd best be getting on back to the house," Martha said. "Edwin will want some supper when he gets home from the lumber mill."

"Take some of this food," Stone said. "Julia cooked more than enough for me."

*

Julia and Martha filled a basket and left. As Martha steered the horse away from the house, Julia glanced over her shoulder and saw that Stone remained standing on the porch. When she turned back around, she saw that Martha was smiling.

"I believe he is smitten," Martha said.

"Smitten?"

Martha nodded. "Yes, with you. I can tell by the way he looks at you."

"I don't know about smitten, but I do know he enjoys my cooking." Julia couldn't ignore the warm feeling that flooded her as she thought about how eagerly he'd looked at the food. And when he touched her, she felt a slight tingling sensation.

"That is a great place to start. Has he shown you his garden?"

Julia nodded. "Yes, it looks big enough to feed a large family and have plenty to can."

"And he has cattle. You would never go hungry if you married Stone."

"I know." Julia sighed as her thoughts went back to the home she'd left. "I am still not sure this is the place for me."

"Only you can decide that." Martha slapped the reins on the horse and pulled to the right. "But you did say you would give it some time, so you should not make too hasty of a decision."

Pastor Ledbetter was at the house waiting for them. His job at the lumber mill supplemented his pastoring, and he said he enjoyed it because it gave him plenty of material for his sermons. Julia marveled at the man's abundant energy.

After he said the blessing, they dug into the food that Julia had prepared. Martha's eyebrows went up. "You truly are a gifted cook. This food is delicious."

"Mama taught my sister Mary and me how to cook when we were little girls. My older sister Lenora moved out when she married, and when I tried to teach my younger sister Sarah, she wasn't interested. I wonder how Daddy is dealing with that."

"I am sure he must miss you at mealtime." The pastor chuckled as he put down his fork. "But remember, Julia, that when people want something badly enough they do what they have to do to get it. When you were there, your sister didn't see any reason to do any of the cooking. Now that you are gone, she will probably step up and take over."

"I hope you are right." Julia took one last bite of peas and put down her fork. "I have to admit it is nice to cook in such a nice kitchen."

Martha turned to her husband and told him about how well appointed Stone's kitchen was. "I would love to have a new stove."

"The one you have still works just fine," Pastor Ledbetter said. "If it ever wears out, we can discuss it."

Martha laughed. "My stove may be old, but I think it will probably last forever."

After everyone finished eating, Julia nudged the pastor and Martha out of the kitchen. "You two go relax. I can clean up."

"If you're sure."

"I'm positive."

Julia was grateful for the time alone so she could think. Some of her best and most logical thoughts happened in the kitchen. As she scrubbed the dishes and wiped everything down, she let her mind wander to what she might do.

Even though she missed her home, she knew things would never be the same if she went back. And in the few short days since she'd been in Colorado, she knew she'd miss Martha.

Stone was on her mind as well. Her initial reaction of anger and frustration had faded quite a bit as she realized what a gentle and caring man he was. But that didn't mean she needed to marry him ... or did it?

*

On Sunday morning, Stone got up extra early. He'd hunted all over town for what he hoped to surprise Julia with.

Martha had given him an idea that grew in his mind after she and Julia left his house.

He fidgeted with his bow tie—something he rarely wore, even to church. But he wanted to look extra nice, knowing that Julia would be there. She's agreed to give Colorado at least a week before heading back home, and he wanted to give her every reason to stay.

After he had his tie as good as he could get it, he combed his hair. Then he went out and hitched his horse to the carriage, hoping he'd convince Julia to come home with him for dinner after church.

He'd asked one of the women on the next ranch over to prepare a meal for him and Julia and have it ready when they returned. She agreed since he'd been so generous with his land after a large portion of hers and her husband's had flooded last year. It was difficult asking for favors, but this was extenuating circumstances, and he wanted this more than he remembered desiring anything in the past.

As soon as he stepped inside the church sanctuary, he noticed several people doing a double take. He had to push back his self-consciousness in order to walk to his regular pew. Then he looked around until he spotted Julia on the front row beside Martha.

She glanced over her shoulder and smiled. Since church hadn't started yet, he squeezed his eyes shut, asked the Lord to be with him as he did something that made him very uncomfortable, got up, and went over to Julia.

"Do you mind if I sit here?" he asked.

Martha's eyes widened as she looked at Julia. "I suppose that would be fine."

As he sat down beside Julia, he glanced over at her hand that rested on the Bible in her lap. He admired her long, slender fingers that he knew were capable of cooking delicious meals, and according to what he'd heard from people in town, comforting crying babies. He wanted her for his wife, now more than when she'd first arrived. There was no doubt in his mind that they could grow to love each other over time.

The pastor approached the pulpit and smiled as he skimmed the congregation. His gaze settled on Stone who had to force himself to take deep breaths.

As they sang hymns, responded to the readings, and listened to the sermon, Stone could feel Julia's presence beside him. He liked the way it felt sitting next to her in church, and during the silent prayer time, he prayed that this wouldn't be the last time.

They stood up after the final hymn. Martha leaned around and told Stone how happy she was he came up and sat with them. Finally, he turned to Julia.

"I would like for you to come to my ranch with me for the afternoon ... that is, if you don't have other plans."

Julia glanced over at Martha who offered a slight nod. Then she turned back to him. "That would be fine."

During the carriage ride to his ranch, Stone couldn't think of much to say. He forced himself to talk about the sermon, the weather, and anything else that popped into his mind—all except what he planned to show her.

*

Julia sensed something brewing in Stone as he drove the horse to his ranch. His demeanor made her nervous, but she didn't want him to know. So she answered his questions and tried to expound on his comments—almost to the point of being awkward.

They finally arrived. He took her by the hand, helped her out of the carriage, and looked down at her.

"I would like to show you something in the garden before we go inside," he said softly.

"Why don't I start dinner first, and then we can go to the garden?"

He smiled. "You don't have to cook today, Julia. Dinner is waiting inside." Still holding one of her hands, he started walking around back, pulling her along.

"Did you already plant the rest of your garden?" This whole scenario felt odd and unsettling, but it didn't seem bad.

"You'll see." When they reached the back of the house, he extended his hand, palm up, to a spot beside the steps leading up to the back porch. "It wasn't easy, but I found something I thought you might like."

She looked in the direction of his gesture and spotted something planted in the ground. It appeared to be a thorny stick, but she instantly knew what it was.

"Ooh, a rose bush." She walked over to it, lightly touched the thorny main branch, and then turned to face him. "Do you know what color the flowers will be?"

"White."

Her eyes widened. "White roses?"

He nodded. "Yes, I understand those are your favorites. I had to visit everyone I knew, but finally someone had this to sell me. Do you like it?"

Her heart flooded with an unfamiliar feeling, and all she wanted to do was run straight into his arms and give him a big kiss. But instead, she remained standing in one spot as a tear found its way down her cheek, and she smiled back at him. "Yes, I do like it. In fact, I love it."

"Since it hasn't bloomed yet, I have to trust that it will yield white roses."

"Stone?" She sniffled and then inhaled deeply.

"You called me Stone."

She smiled, nodded, and swallowed hard. "Can we go inside and have dinner now?"

A concerned look came over him. "Yes, of course."

Throughout dinner, he kept looking at her, and instead of making her uncomfortable, she felt a strange sensation coursing through her veins. Never in her life had anyone gone to such an effort to surprise her, and she was beyond flattered.

Finally, after they ate and cleaned up, she asked if he

would take her to the Ledbetters' house. Without any hesitation, he said he would.

Neither of them spoke the whole way there. Once he pulled up in front of the house, he started to get out, before she touched his arm. He turned to look at her.

"Stone?" Her voice came out in a squeak.

His forehead crinkled. "Did I do something wrong?"

"No," she said as she shook her head. "In fact, I have a question for you."

"I hope I have an answer."

"Do you still want me to stay in Colorado?" When he didn't say anything, her heart sank. "You sent for me to be your bride. Is your offer still open?"

His jaw tightened as he studied her face. "Do you want it to be?"

She closed her eyes, said a prayer that she had read the Lord's message correctly. When she opened her eyes and saw the expectant look on Stone's face, she nodded. "Yes, very much."

Epilogue

Stone paced outside the bedroom door, as the sound of his wife's cries grew weaker. Martha came out with an update.

"Any minute now. We can see the baby's head." Martha disappeared back into the room.

His heart raced as he thought about all that had transpired over the past ten months. Just when he'd thought she was about to return to Virginia, she changed her mind and agreed to remain in Colorado to become his wife. They'd married a week later, and now they had a baby about to make an appearance. Nothing could have made him happier, only he was worried about Julia.

The sound of shuffling and Julia's voice caught his attention. He remained by the door, holding his breath, until he heard the baby crying.

Martha came back to the door and motioned for him to go inside. "I would like to introduce you to your new son."

"Daniel," he whispered. He and Julia had discussed what to name their baby, and if it was a boy, they'd agreed on Daniel, after one of his brothers.

"Isn't he beautiful?" Julia asked as she pulled the blanket from the baby's face.

Stone nodded. "He has your eyes."

She grinned back at him. "And your determination."

Without wasting another second, Stone sat down on the edge of the bed and pulled his family into his arms. He'd never experienced love like this before in his life, and he knew that he would do anything to protect them.

"Stone?"

He leaned away to look into his wife's eyes. "Yes?"

"I love you."

Lenora's Inconvenient Marriage

Hollister Sisters Mail Order Brides

Debby Mayne

Nevertheless let every one of you in particular so love his wife even as himself; and the wife see that she reverence her husband.

Ephesians 5:33

Chapter 1

(April 1883, Virginia)

"Andrew!" Lenora rushed toward her little boy and physically removed him from the counter that he had begun to climb.

His chin quivered as she pulled him closer. "But I want some cake."

Lenora leaned down to look five-year-old Andrew in the eyes. "You cannot have cake until after supper."

"I don't want supper. I hate potatoes." He pulled away, ran across the room, and threw himself on the floor.

He was getting increasingly difficult to handle. Ever since her husband Harvey was murdered, she'd been on her own, trying to be a good mother and provide for herself and her little boy. The last thing she wanted to do was move back home to live with Papa and her baby sister Sarah, but unfortunately she wasn't sure she would have a choice.

Lenora lifted the back of her hand to her forehead as she struggled to fight back the tears. The only foods she could afford anymore were potatoes and onions. The only reason they had cake was that someone from the church had brought it. She was so angry after Harvey was killed that she'd stopped attending church, so she was aware that bringing the cake was a way for the ladies' group to entice her back. If it hadn't been for little Andrew, she would have turned it down.

Her husband Harvey had worked at the bank, and he brought home a nice salary. They managed to save some of it, which was how she had gotten by at first. When money started running low, one of the businessmen in town offered to buy her house and rent it back to her. As much as she didn't want to do that, she needed the cash. Now that money was running low, her only option now was to return to her childhood home.

She glanced over at her little boy who sat on the floor staring up at her. The look on his face broke her heart.

"Mama, I'm hungry."

"I know, sweetheart. I'll start supper now."

He opened his mouth, but after she gave him the glare that was becoming all too common lately, he closed his mouth and lowered his head. It tore her up inside to see his spirit getting so low.

*

(Golden, Colorado)

"You need to find a wife." The church leaders had called Pastor Jesse Grant into a meeting to discuss plans for the next year. "The church needs your attention, and having a woman at home will give you more freedom to do what is needed from a pastor of a church this size."

Jesse shook his head. "I had a wife, and look what happened."

One of the men affectionately placed his hand on Jesse's shoulder. "Yes, and that was a terrible tragedy that would affect anyone. But it has been three years now, and it is time to move forward."

Jesse knew he was right. The fire that had consumed his home and the family he loved with all his heart had long since burned out, but with it went a piece of his soul. He didn't want to remarry and risk going through the pain and heartache again, but even he understood that three years was a long time to be on his own at this stage of life.

He looked around the room and met each man's gaze before speaking in a low tone. "There is one problem you haven't considered. There are very few single women in Colorado, and the ones I know of wouldn't be suitable for a pastor."

The men exchanged looks before one of them placed an envelope in front of him. "That is why we have taken the first step for you."

Jesse frowned as he glanced at the envelope. "What is that?"

"Information about your new bride."

"New bride?" Jesse picked up the envelope, turned it over in his hands, and finally pulled out the paper. "Sarah Hollister? It says here that she is feisty and very young." He shook his head and shoved the paper back across the table toward the men. "No, I'm sorry, but a woman like this wouldn't be right for me. If I ever marry again, the woman must be mature and settled."

The man closest to him stood without picking the envelope back up. "Think about it, Pastor. You don't have to make a decision right now."

Another man nodded. "If you need to discuss this with someone, why don't you talk to your friend Pastor Ledbetter? He will have some words of wisdom that I am sure will help."

After the men left, Jesse picked up the envelope, pulled out the paper, and studied it some more. There was some detailed information about Sarah Hollister who was the youngest of four girls. Her father had written the letter, stating that the family had fallen on hard times since he'd become a widower, and he couldn't afford to continue feeding his daughter who remained at home.

He put down the letter, leaned back, and closed his eyes. First, he wondered what had prompted his church leaders to correspond with Mr. Hollister. And then he started thinking about the widowed man with the daughters. The words he used spoke of love and anguish about his situation. He must have been desperate to write such a letter.

Jesse's first inclination was to tear up the letter and toss it, but now he felt compelled to respond. He went to his desk, pulled out some paper, and started writing to let Mr. Hollister know he wasn't interested in marrying someone so young but he'd be praying for a suitable man to come into her life.

*

(Virginia)

Lenora knew that she wouldn't be able to pay more than another month's rent, and then she'd be out of money. She was left with no choice but to move back in with Papa. As much as she hated to do this, she had to do it for Andrew.

It would be difficult to be back under her father's care, with his scrutinizing eyes and strict manner. But it wouldn't be terrible. Andrew adored her younger sister Sarah who still lived with their father. Her playfulness never ceased to make Andrew squeal with delight.

She took Andrew by the hand and led him toward the door of the house they could no longer afford. He gave her a questioning look and pulled back. "Come on, Andrew. Let's go."

"Where are we going, Mama?"

"To see Aunt Sarah."

His eyes instantly lit up. "I can't wait to see Aunt Sarah. Do you think she has candy for me?"

Lenora laughed. "I have no idea."

"Maybe she will play marbles with me." He pulled free and started running around the house.

"What are you doing?"

He paused long enough to glance over his shoulder. "Looking for my marbles."

"Maybe she'll let you play with hers. We don't have time to dilly dally."

He skipped over to her and took her by the hand singing, "I'm going to see Aunt Sarah. She plays with me. She is so much fun."

Lenora couldn't help but laugh as they walked down the street toward her family home. Sarah was the only person who brought such joy to her little boy, and it made Lenora happy to see him in such a good mood.

Sarah greeted her at the door with a smile and open arms for Andrew who remained standing by Lenora's side. "Where on earth have you been, little peanut?" She scooped her little nephew into her arms and swung him around. "I have missed you so much!"

He giggled as she put him down. "Do it again, Aunt Sarah."

She shot a playful look in Lenora's direction and then looked back down at Andrew. "One more time, and that's all. You're almost too big for this."

She swung him around a little bit longer this time. When she put him back on the floor, he wrapped both of his arms around her legs. "I love you, Aunt Sarah."

"I love you too, peanut, but you're almost big enough to pick me up."

Lenora grinned at her sister as she walked farther into the house. "Don't give him any ideas."

Sarah clasped her hands together as she continued smiling at Lenora. "So how have you two been?"

Lenora's smile faded. There was no point in trying to pretend anymore. "Not good."

"No one is sick are they?" Sarah looked down at Andrew and then at Lenora. "What's wrong?"

"It's a long story, so why don't we make some tea and sit

at the kitchen table?"

It took Lenora the better part of an hour to explain how dire her circumstances had become. Sarah listened with rapt attention, shaking her head as she heard what Lenora had never expected to say.

"It pains me to do this, but I don't see that I have any other choice but to move back here." Lenora glanced around at the meager furnishings. "I'll bring my furniture, of course."

The expression on Sarah's face concerned her. For the first time Lenora could remember, her youngest sister wasn't smiling and jovial.

"Did I say something wrong?" Lenora asked.

Sarah shook her head. "No, it's just that ..." She sighed. "Papa isn't exactly his old self anymore. After marrying Julia off, he's starting to work on me."

"But why? You are still young. You have plenty of time to find a husband."

"He is having a difficult time making ends meet. For the first time I can ever remember, he told me that if I can't find a job or husband, he will have to find one for me."

Lenora gasped. "But you're not ready!" As soon as those words escaped her lips, she regretted them. "What I mean is—"

Sarah offered a half-smile and nodded. "I know what you mean, and I agree. I don't want to get married, and I have no idea what kind of job I would be qualified to do ... unless someone wants me to come play with their children."

"You could do what Mary is doing."

"They require too much from her. Even Mary is growing tired of all that they ask her to do."

Lenora stared at her sister for a few seconds before nodding. Sarah had never been one to work hard, and she got away with it because of her extremely sweet disposition. Everyone around her wanted to see her warm and infectious smile, so they did everything they could to keep her happy.

"Maybe you can become a governess," Sarah said. "It would come natural to you."

"I'm afraid that would be difficult since I can barely keep up with my own child." Lenora let out a long sigh. "I will think of something."

Sarah's contemplative expression quickly faded, and her eyes began to sparkle again. "We can talk to Papa and hear what he has to say. I don't think he will tell you no flat out." She clapped her hands together. "It will be so much fun to have you and Andrew living here!"

Lenora cast a half-smile at her sister. "You just want me here to cook so you can play with Andrew."

Sarah grinned back. "There is that."

The sound of their father's footsteps coming toward the house quieted them. When he opened the door, he had an odd look on his face.

Chapter 2

(Colorado)

Two weeks later, Jesse said goodbye to the last of the people leaving the church after services. He'd been invited to several people's homes for Sunday dinner, but he turned them all down.

After the group of men had come to him about the mail order bride, several people made remarks about how important it was to have a wife, so he was well aware that his marital status was being discussed. He didn't feel like listening to more people harping on something he had no intention of doing.

He went home to an empty house and headed straight to the pantry to prepare something to eat. It was a lonely existence, but he didn't interfere with anyone else's life, unless it pertained to their spirituality, and even then, he only did what he had to do. When his wife Viola was alive, he had a thriving ministry, with all kinds of activities and excitement that made him happy to wake up every single morning. Now, though, he dreaded each day that was even more miserable than the last.

He remembered that one of the men who'd come with the letter recommended talking to Edwin Ledbetter. Ironically, Edwin was only person Jesse could talk to, but it wasn't always easy since they were both in the ministry. However, he just happened to know that later this evening would be a good time. Last time they spoke, they'd discussed how busy they were with their flocks, and Edwin had mentioned that every week after Sunday socializing, he and his wife often relaxed in their home.

Jesse waited until he thought enough time had passed after church services were over before unhitching his horse and taking off toward the other side of Golden, where Edwin and his wife lived. The small town was thriving, and the land was there for the taking. Most of it could still be purchased for a fraction of the price of land back East, which attracted even more people looking for an opportunity to get rich.

It obviously worked for many of them. Jesse knew more rich folks in Colorado in the ten years he'd lived here than he'd known all his life before. In fact, as he and Viola worked toward building the church, he worked in the goldmines until the church could support itself. Now he had enough money that he'd never have to worry about finances for the remainder of his life. But that didn't matter to him because he didn't have his wife and children to share it with him.

As he rounded the last patch of trees and came upon the clearing with Edwin's house and church, he let out a deep sigh. Although Edwin's church wasn't as large as his, he had so much more to be thankful for—namely his wife. They didn't have children, but they had each other.

Edwin was standing outside, shielding his eyes from the late afternoon sun. When he recognized Jesse, he grinned and waved.

"Martha told me she heard someone approaching." He closed the gap between them. "It sure is good to see you, Jesse. What brings you here?"

"It will take me a while to explain. I hope you and Martha aren't busy."

"Naw, we generally take Sunday afternoons to enjoy the Lord's blessings." Edwin stepped aside and gestured toward the house. "Why don't you come on inside, and I'll get Martha to put on a pot of tea."

Once seated, it took Jesse a while to work up the courage to tell Edwin and Martha what had taken place. "I don't know what gave the leaders of my church the impression that I would be even remotely interested in a mail order bride."

Edwin and Martha exchanged a glance before Edwin spoke up. "I suppose I should tell you that they came to me first. They were concerned about you and how lonely you have become, so I told them about some of our successes with mail order brides. Martha just happened to know about the sister of one of our members."

Martha nodded. "Did the letter come from Mr. Hollister?"

Jesse slowly nodded. "I never would have thought you would be involved in something like this, Edwin." No wonder the men had recommended talking to Edwin.

"It isn't a sin to want a companion, you know," the older pastor said softly. "The Lord created man and woman to be partners."

"Yes, I realize that, but I have already had my family. I don't need a woman now."

Martha smiled softly. "Would you please at least consider getting to know someone? When Julia Hollister arrived, she was distraught over the very thought of being a mail order bride, and ..." She turned to her husband who smiled before she looked back at Jesse. "And now, she is one of the happiest women I know."

Jesse wasn't getting the support he'd hoped for. In fact, he had a sinking sensation that there was no one who would understand how he felt.

"I don't think I can love another woman after losing

Viola." Jesse's throat constricted, causing him to choke on his words.

Martha hopped up, got him a drink of water, and sat back down. "I know it will be hard at first, but why don't you allow the Lord to work His miracles? If you decide to invite a woman to visit, you don't have to marry her if you don't think she would be a good helpmate to you."

"Wouldn't that be a terrible thing to do to a woman?" he asked. "Especially knowing that I'm not likely to be interested in her?"

Edwin shook his head. "No, not at all. In fact, there are so many men here, if you choose not to marry her, she is likely to have them standing in line for her. She will have plenty to choose from." He chuckled. "I would think this would be a wonderful opportunity for a woman who doesn't mind living in the West."

Jesse had to admit that if he didn't have to marry the woman, the situation didn't seem as preposterous as he'd originally thought. But then he remembered the letter he had sent back to Mr. Hollister.

"I told him that Sarah was too young for me." Jesse glanced down at the table and then up at Martha. "Perhaps I acted too quickly."

She slowly shook her head. "If you feel that she is too young, you can wait for someone who is a little bit older."

"Not too old, though," Edwin said. "She needs to be young enough to bear children."

"But—" Jesse began before Edwin lifted a finger.

"You might not want children again, but if you choose not to marry her, she will need to be able to have children for someone else." Edwin grinned. "I'm sure you understand that."

Jesse cleared his throat. "Yes, of course I do."

Martha hopped up from the table again. "I hope you can stay for supper. It's not much, but you need to eat something before you head back to your place."

After a relaxing dinner, Jesse went back home with a completely different attitude about sending for a mail order bride. He had no idea what to do next, but he had no doubt the men in his congregation would have some ideas.

*

(Virginia)

Lenora knew that Papa would never be able to turn her away. But once she and Andrew moved back home, she could tell that he was worried now more than ever. She gave him the small amount of money she had to help with food. He reluctantly accepted it, but it was painfully obvious that doing so hurt his pride.

Sarah, on the other hand, seemed to love having her and Andrew in the house. Lenora cheerfully did all of the housework and cooking, knowing that her son was in the loving care of her sweet sister.

A little more than a month after she and Andrew moved in, Papa came home in a mood she had never seen before. Sarah's eyes clouded over as soon as she saw him.

The instant Papa went to his room to freshen up for supper, Sarah pulled Lenora away from Andrew. "It's happening again."

"What is happening?"

Sarah shook her head. "This is the way he acted when he got that letter from the man who sent for Julia."

"Does he expect you to go out West?" Before Sarah had a chance to answer, Lenora continued. "I don't want to stand in your way of getting married, but I'm afraid Andrew will miss you terribly if you leave."

"I don't want to be a mail order bride." Sarah grimaced. "But neither did Julia, and last I heard from her, she is very happy." Some of the light had faded from her eyes.

Lenora's heart ached for her younger sister. The very thought of being sent away to marry some man she'd never even met must be terrifying for Sarah. She was certain it was bad enough for Julia who had always been the strongest sister.

"If you don't want to go, I'll do everything in my power to help you stay."

Sarah's chin quivered as she nodded. "You're a wonderful big sister. I am so blessed."

Papa chose that moment to come out of his room. He grinned back and forth between his daughters. "I am so happy to see the two of you getting along so well."

Lenora cast a quick glance at Sarah who stood there staring at Papa. He finally pulled the envelope out of his pocket and slapped it on the kitchen table.

"What is that, Papa?" Lenora asked. Out of the corner of her eyes, she could see Sarah's sullen face.

He lifted his chin to face Lenora head on. "This is your ticket to Colorado."

Lenora turned to Sarah with a sympathetic smile. "You were right, Sarah. You have been sent for."

"No," Papa said. "This is for you, Lenora. He wasn't interested in Sarah ... said she was too young, so I wrote him and told him about you."

"B-but—" Lenora's heart sank. "I can't go. What about Andrew?"

"His ticket is in here too. He wants the both of you as a package deal, provided, of course, the two of you can hit it off."

"I'm sorry, Papa, but this isn't what I want."

His shoulders sagged lower than they already were. "It's not what I want either, Lenora. It wasn't what I wanted when Julia left either. But I can't see any other way." His shoulders drooped even more. "You know that I love all four of you girls more than life itself. If I had the means, I would never let any of you leave the house. Unfortunately, I cannot think of anything else to do."

"There has to be a way." Lenora looked at Sarah,

pleading with her eyes. "I have to find a way to stay here."

"I am so sorry, Lenora." Papa's voice cracked. "One thing he made very clear was that if you don't get along with him or his congregation, there will be no marriage."

"Congregation?"

"Yes. He's a pastor. Apparently, it's a rather large church—bigger than the one your sister attends."

"It's in Colorado?" Lenora asked as she picked up the envelope.

Papa nodded. "Yes, it is in Golden, Colorado, a little bit more than an hour by horse from Julia."

Sarah's eyebrows shot up as she leaned forward. "I want to go."

Lenora spun around to face her. "You want to marry this man?"

"No, silly, I just want to go see Julia."

Chapter 3

Lenora sat next to Andrew on the train, holding his hand, praying that this journey would be an adventure that they wouldn't look back on with regret. As soon as Andrew found out he'd be riding on a train, he hooted with joy. Lenora, on the other hand, dreaded the long trip that could lead her to a horrible place.

The only reason she conceded was that Julia was there and had agreed to be at the station when she arrived. She was grateful that the man who had sent for her and Andrew was generous enough to send money in addition to the ticket. She split it with Papa, knowing he worried about having enough food for himself and Sarah.

"Mama, when will we be there?" Andrew asked about an hour into the trip.

"Not for several days, sweetheart."

"When will we eat?" He looked at her with fear in his eyes. "Where will we sleep?"

"Right here." She forced a smile as she pulled him closer. "You may sleep whenever you like."

He whimpered for a few minutes but finally relaxed and allowed Lenora to snuggle him. Within seconds, he was fast asleep.

*

The train ride was one of most difficult experiences Lenora had endured, but it was nothing compared to the months that had followed Harvey's death. Andrew didn't remember much about his father, but he asked quite a few questions during the trip. That was another reason Lenora wanted the trip to be over.

They had just gotten notice that their stop was coming up soon when Andrew turned to Lenora with his eyes open wide. "Mama, will we have to ride on this train again to go back home?"

She swallowed hard. "We will if we decide to go back … home."

He frowned. "I don't want to. It takes too long."

"I know, sweetheart, I know." She pulled him closer and gave him a long hug.

Andrew was the only thing keeping her from crumpling, and she was willing to protect him with her life. The biggest motivation for agreeing to meet this man who had sent for her was the possibility of a future without hunger for her son. Papa couldn't guarantee that.

As the train pulled to a stop at the station, she scanned the faces of the people waiting on the platform. The instant she spotted Julia, her heart hammered. It had been a couple of years since she had seen her sister, and it delighted her to no end to be this close again.

"Look, Andrew." She pointed out the window toward the woman who looked like a much happier version of the sister who always appeared so miserable. "There is your Aunt Julia."

He grinned as he spotted Julia. "I remember her. She is the one who always looked like she was eating lemons." He turned to Lenora. "But she doesn't now."

"I think she is happy because she has a nice husband and a couple of children to love."

Andrew looked Lenora in the eyes. "Is that why you are always so happy? You have me to love?"

Lenora smiled and nodded as she tousled Andrew's hair. "Yes, sweetheart, you make me very happy."

*

Jesse stood back and waited. He'd come to the train station with an entourage of people who supported him and agreed to be there when the woman arrived.

Julia went right up front to greet her sister, while Edwin and Martha hung back with him. A couple of the lay leaders from the church were also there since they had been the ones to come to him about the mail order bride scheme in the first place.

As much as he tried not to appear fazed by the situation, his insides roiled. He was conflicted with a combination of emotions, from anticipation and curiosity to dread and worry. What if he didn't like her, or worse, what if she didn't like him? What if her little boy was a problem?

He remembered his own children and how difficult they could be at times. But they were his, so he loved them with all his heart in spite of their behavior. Would he be able to love this woman's child as his own?

"Here she comes!" Julia jumped up and down until an attractive woman holding the hand of a little boy stepped off the train.

He studied the pair of them and realized she looked quite a bit like Julia. The two of them hugged before Julia held her sister out at arm's length. And they both burst into a fit of giggles and hugged again. The little boy remained standing there, looking around, appearing confused by everything.

Finally, Julia let go of her sister, bent down, and hugged the child. He hugged her back, hanging on even after she let go. She laughed again and whispered something that made him smile.

Lenora said something to Julia, who turned around and gestured for Jesse to join them. With a pounding heart and dry mouth, he began a slow walk toward the sisters.

"Pastor Grant," Julia said as she tugged at his arm. "I would like for you to meet my sister Lenora Baucom."

"Mrs. Baucom, it is very nice to meet you." He forced himself to smile down at the little boy. "And you must be Andrew."

The child's eyes widened. He glanced up at his mother, who nodded. "It's … it's nice to meet you too, sir."

Jesse was familiar with the fear he saw in the little boy's eyes. He knew he had a commanding presence, being over six feet tall, fully bearded, and rather portly. He wouldn't harm a fly, but other people didn't know that about him.

Julia cast a curious glance at her nephew and then at Jesse before turning back to Lenora. "You will be staying with us … at least for a while … until …" She let out a nervous giggle. "Until you're not."

As Lenora smiled at Julia, a bolt of emotion shot through his heart. She was every bit as pretty as Julia and had a much warmer demeanor … until she looked at him. That was when he saw the shield go up.

Edwin and Martha stepped toward them. Lenora spoke softly to the other pastor and his wife as Julia introduced them, but he couldn't hear what she had to say.

"I thought we could go to your church now so Lenora can meet some folks from your congregation before she and her son head on back with Julia," Edwin said.

It was a very awkward situation, but he didn't expect it to be otherwise. Now that he was here with all of these people making decisions for him, Jesse thought it might have been better if he had come alone. At least they could have had some uninterrupted conversation.

"Would you like for Lenora to ride with you?" Julia asked. "I can take Andrew with me."

The little boy's face turned pale as he clung to his mother's arm. Jesse wasn't sure what to do, so he did nothing.

Julia leaned over and whispered something to him again. Andrew reluctantly let go of his mother and took his aunt's hand.

Lenora gave him an apologetic smile. "I'm afraid my son is overwhelmed by everything."

"Yes, it certainly appears that way." Jesse wanted to kick himself for his tone coming across so gruff, but Andrew wasn't the only one who was overwhelmed. This was difficult for Jesse too, with everyone staring at him as he met the woman who just might become his wife.

Her smile faded as she spoke to her sister. A few minutes later, Jesse helped Lenora into his carriage, and they were on their way to the church.

Neither of them said a word at first, so a few miles up the road, he decided to break the ice. "Did you have a nice train ride?"

"It was okay for me, but Andrew became weary by the end of the first day." She sighed. "I suppose I should have known that would be the case since he is so young."

"He needs to learn to be a man." Jesse didn't look at Lenora as they spoke. He didn't want her to see the pain he felt when talking about her child. "We are in the West, and boys have to grow up fast here."

Lenora let out a soft gasp, but she didn't say anything. He cast a brief glance in her direction, and that was when he saw the regret on her face.

*

This man certainly wasn't what Lenora had expected. All of the pastors she'd known had been gentle, soft-spoken men. This one was big and burly and gruff ... so much so he'd frightened sweet little Andrew out of his mind. Lenora was glad Julia had offered to take him rather than subject him to a long ride with the pastor.

"Do you cook?" he asked.

"What?" There had been such a long silence she wasn't prepared for conversation.

"I said, 'Do you cook?'"

She nodded. "Yes, I can cook, although probably not as well as my sister. Julia and I used to spend quite a bit of time in the kitchen with our mother, but I just stayed long enough to get the basics."

"As long as you can do the basics, I suppose that will do." He cleared his throat. "Do you keep a clean house?"

Now Lenora was annoyed. What was this man doing? She knew this would be a marriage of convenience—that is, if it resulted in a marriage at all. But he could have been a little more polite and at least pretended to be interested in her as a woman.

"Well?" he asked, his voice demanding and urgent.

"I do keep a very clean house. But I have never had much to clean, so it has never been that difficult." Before he asked her any more annoying questions, she decided to turn the table. "How about you? What do you do besides pastor a church?"

His eyebrows slammed together as he gave her a look that would have sent her crawling beneath the seat if she'd been younger. But she was a grown woman with a child, and that gave her the confidence, knowing that she had to do whatever it took to make sure Andrew had a decent life.

"Well?" she asked, mimicking his tone.

"I have a ranch." He audibly took in a deep breath and slowly let it out. "Most of the people here have a ranch."

"What do you have on your ranch?"

His features scrunched up as he cast another disapproving look at her. "Cattle, chickens, and horses. I have a garden too."

"I would think so." She smoothed her dress over her lap. "I enjoy gardening."

"I don't garden for pleasure. I do it to eat."

She let out a chuckle that she instantly regretted when he scowled at her. "You can do both, you know. Work doesn't have to be miserable if you do it with the right attitude." She forced a smile. "But of course you would know about that since you are a man of the cloth."

His frown deepened. After he didn't respond, she decided any conversation at this point was futile. He clearly didn't like her, and she wasn't about to be anything other than herself—not after leaving everything she knew behind and spending so long on the train.

They arrived at the church, which was much larger than Lenora had expected. Julie and Andrew had already arrived. People swarmed around the yard, and there was a line to get into the building.

Chapter 4

"Are all of these people members of your church?" Lenora asked.

Jesse shrugged. "Most of them. However, some of the people came from Edwin's church to meet you."

"This is all for me?" She turned completely toward him.

"Actually, for both of us. It seems that a bunch of folks got together and set this whole thing up, and they want to make sure we don't mess up all of their plans."

"Well, that explains a lot." Lenora gathered her skirt and hopped down from the carriage. "I suppose I'd better not disappoint anyone. Time to go meet and greet."

Without giving him a chance to give one of his brusque responses, Lenora charged toward the crowd where she spotted her sister standing off to the side, chatting with another couple. A man stood next to her, and several children, including Andrew, played off to the side.

Julia spun around and opened her arms wide. "Come, Lenora! I want you to meet my husband." She pulled Lenora closer. "Stone, this is the beautiful sister I've been telling you about."

Stone gave her a smile as wide as his face. "Indeed, I

have heard so many wonderful things about you, Lenora, I feel as though I know you already. I am so happy you have decided to make this trip."

Lenora was surprised by how friendly and open Stone was, after experiencing the surliness of Jesse. "I am delighted to be here."

He burst into laughter and then lowered his voice. "I appreciate your attempt to be gracious, but I suspect you're already having regrets."

Julia leaned over and whispered, "I already told him how exhausted you were. He promised he'd see to it that this thing didn't last too long so you could come home and get some rest."

"Thank you." Lenora tried to smile, but she couldn't. Instead, a tear found its way to the corner of her eye. She tried to wipe it without anyone noticing, but Julia saw her.

"Oh, Lenora, you are too tired for this now, aren't you?" Julia sighed. "I mentioned that we might want to wait, but you know how people are. They're so curious about the new person in town."

"That's okay. I'll try to muddle through it." She glanced over her shoulder to check on Andrew. "Looks like he managed to jump right in."

Julia laughed. "He didn't exactly have a choice. A couple of the boys came and started throwing a ball to him, and he had to catch it, or it would have hit him in the face." She paused and put her arm around Lenora. "I bet that's how you feel about this—that it's hitting you in the face."

"That's a pretty good analogy." Lenora took a step toward the church. "So this is the church where Jesse is pastor?"

"Yes. Isn't it lovely? He is the second pastor here. The first one got out of the ministry. Jesse came here with his wife, and they started having children right away, so they were starting to build a new house to fit their growing family. Unfortunately, the house they lived in temporarily burned to the ground, and he lost his wife and both children."

"That is very sad," Lenora said as she thought about his churlish nature. "It is enough to make a person feel as though there is nothing left."

"You would know the feeling," Julia agreed. "But I see a big difference between you and Pastor Grant."

Lenora gave her sister a curious look. "What's that?"

"Ironically, you are the one leaning on the Lord, while he seems to be wallowing in self-pity. Seems it should be the other way around." Julia tilted her head. "After all, he is a pastor."

"But he is still a man," Lenora reminded her.

"True. That is why he needs a wife." Julia lowered her voice. "And if you don't want to marry him, you don't have to. Stone says you and Andrew can stay with us as long as you need to."

"I don't want to impose."

Julia flipped her hand from the wrist. "You won't be imposing at all. When you see the size of our house, you'll worry about getting lost and finding us. That thing is huge."

Lenora smiled. "Is it bigger than our house back home?"

"You could put several of our houses back home into the one Stone built before I ever met him."

"I'm looking forward to seeing it."

Andrew came running toward them, practically knocking his mother over before he stopped. "Mama, I like the children here. They don't leave me out."

"That is good, Andrew, because this is likely to be where we go to church." That reminded Lenora of a question she'd thought of when she first heard that she would be staying an hour away. "Will I go to your church while I stay with you, or will I go here?"

Julia pursed her lips. "That is a sore spot with me. I wanted you to go to our church—at least until you are comfortable around Pastor Grant. But his church leaders are insisting you come here."

"That's fine. I really don't mind. But how will I get here?"

"Someone will come and get you. If they can't, I can let you take one of our carriages ... but only after you learn your way around."

"I don't want her coming alone," Jesse said as he approached. "I will come get her."

Lenora looked at him and then at her sister whose eyes had widened before responding. "I would never want to inconvenience anyone."

Jesse shook his head. "It doesn't matter. If there is ever a time that I can't drive you here, I will find someone who can."

"Okay," Lenora said.

"You need to go inside with me. There are some women you need to meet."

Lenora saw that Julia noticed his gruff nature by the way her sister grimaced. "Okay, let's go."

He cast a quick disapproving glance at both of them before turning his back to lead her to the church. Julia made a face, making Lenora laugh.

"I'll keep an eye on Andrew," Julia said. "Go on and do whatever you have to do."

Once inside, it took a few moments for her eyes to adjust to the indoors after standing in the bright sun. A group of older women sat at a table, having tea and chatting. One of them saw her and shushed the group.

"Here she comes," one of the women said as she gestured toward Lenora and Jesse.

He walked her to the table, announced her name, and then left her alone with the women. It seemed terribly rude of him, but she was here now, and she fully intended to make the most of it.

"Have a seat, Lenora," the woman at the head of the table said. "My name is Catherine, and these ladies are Myrtle, Josephine, Anne, Beatrice, Margaret, Melanie, Clara, and Abigail."

The last lady, Abigail, offered a warm smile. "Don't

worry, dear. We will give you plenty of time to learn our names. But right now, we would like to get to know you better. Would you like something to drink?"

Lenora sat down. "No, thank you."

Catherine spoke up again. "We understand that you are here to marry our pastor. He is a very quiet man who has been alone for a number of years since his family perished. I want to warn you that it might not be easy to warm his heart."

"I understand. I lost my husband shortly after Andrew was born. It is very difficult and heartbreaking."

"Tell us about Andrew," another woman said. "Does he get along well with other children?"

"Yes … at least back home he did—that is, when he was around them."

The ladies all exchanged glances before Catherine asked another question. "Is he obedient? We feel that it is important for a pastor's children to be obedient."

"Most of the time," Lenora said with a smile that was only returned by a couple of the women. "But I do have to remember that he is a little boy and very full of energy. In fact, on the trip here—"

Catherine interrupted her. "We expect our pastor's wife to be involved in all of the ladies' group events."

Lenora tilted her head as she directed her response to Catherine. "That is understandable. What all do you ladies do?"

Catherine didn't seem pleased by Lenora's question, but before she could say another word, Abigail responded. "We do things for each other, like cook when someone is sick …" She glanced around the table, and everyone nodded.

"We have church picnics," Clara added. "And we do quilting."

"Yes," Abigail agreed, "we do quite a bit of sewing."

"That sounds delightful," Lenora said. "Of course, I am not certain that I will be the pastor's wife. We've barely met."

The women all looked at each other before turning to face her. "You must marry him," Catherine said flatly. "We cannot have a pastor who is as lonely as he has become."

"Are you saying—?" Lenora began before Catherine cut her off.

"What we are saying is that if Pastor Grant doesn't find a wife soon, we will have to put out another call to find someone else to lead us." Catherine leaned back in her chair and folded her arms. "Being married is not typically a requirement of a pastor, but we feel that in this case, it is in his best interest ... and in ours as a congregation."

Lenora's chin dropped. She had no idea what to say or if she should say anything. All she knew was that a lot of people were watching her and checking to see if she was marriage material for Jesse Grant. Unfortunately, they didn't take a long enough look at him to see that he might not be ready for such a commitment. But this wasn't the time or place to mention any of that.

They asked her a couple more questions before Catherine leaned back. "You may go now. I imagine you must be tired after traveling so far."

"I am."

Abigail stood. "Let me walk you back out to Pastor Grant."

As soon as they left the church building, Abigail stopped and touched Lenora on the shoulder. "Don't let them get to you, dear. They mean well, but there is no way they can possibly know what is on your heart."

"Thank you."

"You seem like a sweet person who cares deeply about others. Pastor Grant used to be that way too, but ever since his family died, he has become more difficult to deal with. That is why so many people think he needs a wife."

Lenora allowed her shoulders to relax. Abigail was such a sweet woman she felt as though she could become a close friend and confidante. But she still needed to be cautious. "I want to do the right thing," Lenora said. "I also have to consider my son who is at an age when he needs a man in his life."

"Since you are staying with your sister, you will have Stone Michaels." Abigail smiled. "I can't think of a better man for him to learn from."

That was reassuring. Lenora thanked Abigail again before walking down the church steps and finding Julia.

"How was it?" Julia asked.

"Not too bad." Lenora shrugged. "They just had a lot of questions."

Julia's gaze darted behind Lenora. "Pastor Grant is coming our way."

Chapter 5

As soon as Lenora left with her sister's family, Jesse joined some of the leaders of the church. "What did you think?" Lester asked.

"She seems like a nice woman, but her child is very spirited."

"He is five years old," Lester reminded him. "Boys that age generally are."

"Maybe it would have been better to find a woman without a child."

"Do you remember that we tried? You said she was too young."

Jesse hung his head as he pondered what was going on. Even if he eventually chose not to marry Lenora, he still needed to give her a chance. He raised his gaze. "I will get to know her and make a decision soon."

Lester patted Jesse on the shoulder. "That is all we can ask. She will be coming back for church on Sunday. I will ask Abigail if we can have the two of you over for supper one night before then."

"Will you invite her son?"

"Do you want us to?" Lester paused. "On second thought, perhaps it would be best to leave Lenora's son with her sister so you can get to know her better."

"Yes, I think that would be a good idea."

Later that night, Jesse sat on the edge of his bed, lowered his head, and asked the Lord to give him wisdom to do the right thing. *I don't know if I can ever love another woman, but if I can, I pray for You to make it very obvious.*

When he opened his eyes, he thought about his prayer. He'd gone through the grieving process long enough now. It was time to move on. But could he do it as the church leaders wanted him to?

*

Julia came into Lenora's bedroom two days later. "You have a visitor," she said softly as she pulled back the curtains at the window in the tiny room.

"Jesse?" Lenora sat up in bed.

Julia laughed. "Who else?"

Lenora rubbed her sleepy eyes. "What does he want?"

"All I know is that he showed up at the edge of the property and talked to Stone. And then he came to the house."

"Where is he now?" Lenora got up and started going through the wardrobe Stone had made for her.

"He is having coffee in the kitchen. Take your time. I'll chat with him until you are ready to see him."

Lenora hated making anyone wait, so she quickly got dressed, brushed her hair, and went to see what Jesse wanted. When he saw her, he stood up until she sat down. At least he could be a gentleman when he wanted to.

Julia poured Lenora some coffee before putting the pot back on the stove and straightening her skirt. "I'll go check on the children. If you need anything, just holler."

Once they were alone, Jesse fidgeted with the spoon beside his coffee mug. "I … um …" He looked very uncomfortable as his gaze met hers. "One of the couples from church has asked me if we could go to their house for supper tomorrow night. Is this something you would like to do?"

Lenora nodded. "Yes, that would be very nice."

"They said we can come early so they can get to know you before we eat."

"That is fine." Lenora took a sip of her coffee. "Do I need to bring something?"

His eyebrows came together for a few seconds before he shrugged. "I don't know. My wife always did. Generally when I go to people's house now, though, I don't even think about bringing something, but I'm not sure what to do in this case."

Lenora grinned. "Then I will bring something small. My mama taught me to always bring something when visiting."

Without another word, Jesse stood. "I reckon I'd better get back to the church. It's a long ride, and I have to start preparing my sermon for Sunday."

"But it is only Tuesday."

"Yes, but I like to prepare it so I can think about it later and make changes as things come up. When I have waited until the last minute, I never feel prepared."

Lenora nodded. "I suppose that is the smart thing to do."

He smiled down at her, and for the first time she saw some light in his eyes. "Thank you, Lenora. I will be here at 3:00 tomorrow afternoon." He left without another word.

A few minutes later, Julia came back into the kitchen. "He wasn't here long. What did he want to talk to you about?"

Lenora told her everything. "He never mentioned anything about Andrew."

"Then leave Andrew here with me. He has been such a big help with the little ones." Julia grinned. "They adore him."

"And I am sure he enjoys every bit of that adoration."
*

Jesse had forgotten to tell Lenora that the invitation was just for the two of them. As he drove the carriage to her sister's house, he thought of various ways to let her know.

When he arrived, Julia was outside watching the children play. He pointed to the oldest of the three children. "Is that Lenora's boy?"

"Yes." Julia stood and walked closer to him. "I'm happy to have him here with me to help with the little ones while you and Lenora go to supper. I hope it is okay to leave him here."

"I am sure it is." At least he didn't have to worry about that now. "Where is Lenora? I told her I would be here at 3:00."

"She is inside getting ready. It isn't 3:00 yet." She offered a comforting smile. "Would you like to go inside or stay out here with me? The children can be quite entertaining."

He thought for a moment. "I suppose I can stay out here."

"Hey Daniel!" The sound of Andrew's voice caught their attention. "See if you can catch this ball." He gently rolled the ball toward the little boy who was a couple of years younger.

When Daniel caught it, he stood up and grinned. "Ball," he said. "Catch ball."

"That's very good." Andrew glanced over at his aunt, and she nodded her approval. "Now it is Bethany's turn."

"He seems to be a good boy," Jesse said.

Julia cut a glance in Jesse's direction. "Andrew is very good with the little ones."

Jesse stood and watched as Andrew patiently gave each of his younger cousins a turn to catch the ball. Daniel looked to be around two, and his little sister who could barely walk appeared to be a year or so younger. His own two children were older than these three when they died, but he remembered when they were toddlers.

"It must be difficult," Julia said softly. "I can't even begin to imagine what you have been through."

"It is difficult. I don't think anyone will ever understand."

"Did you know that Stone lost his family in a fire before he came here?"

Jesse lifted his gaze and shook his head. "No, I wasn't aware of that."

"His parents and brothers all perished when his home back East burned to the ground. He had wanted to come west, but he didn't want to leave his family. After they died, he didn't have a reason to stay."

Jesse didn't know Stone Michaels very well, but the few times he'd seen the man, he seemed rather jovial—not like someone who had been through such a horrible tragedy. He had obviously done quite well for himself. The amount of acreage he owned and stone house indicated financial success.

"He didn't like talking about it," Julia continued. "But over time, I have learned more about his family. I wish I could have met his brothers. Listening to Stone talk about them, one would think they could do no wrong."

Jesse let out a soft chuckle. "It is amazing how we only remember the good when we look back."

"I know. But I am sure they were wonderful people. All I have to do is watch Stone, and I can see that he was raised by caring, loving people."

Those words hit Jesse hard. "That is very astute."

"It's true. Anyone who can love the way he does must have learned it from somewhere. I know it all comes from the Lord, and He uses our families to show His love."

"Yes, indeed." Jesse knew that Julia's words would linger in his mind and they'd give him plenty to think about later.

"Maybe I can have Stone talk to you about it."

"No, he doesn't need to talk about it." The last thing he wanted to do was discuss what he'd been through. Even if Stone only spoke of his own personal experience, it would cause Jesse to have to relive losing his wife and children.

He glanced over at the porch and saw that Lenora was

standing there, watching. When she noticed that he saw her, she came down to the yard.

"Don't worry about Andrew," Julia said. "He will be just fine." She cut a glance to Jesse. "Be good to my sister."

That last comment startled Jesse. No one had spoken to him like that since before he went into the ministry. "Of course I will."

Julia gave him a playful grin. "Just making sure."

They got into the carriage, and he steered the horse toward the road. Once they were on their way, Lenora spoke up. "I hope you don't mind my sister. She is very protective."

"I thought you were older."

She nodded. "I am, but she has always acted older. When we were younger, she was home more than I was … and then I married young."

"Do you still miss him?" The instant those words left Jesse's mouth, he regretted saying them.

"Are you talking about my husband?"

"Yes, but if it makes you too uncomfortable, you don't have to answer."

"No, I want to answer. And yes, of course, I do miss him … especially at night. We used to have long conversations late at night, talking about our dreams and hopes for the future. He wanted a large family, and I'd planned on making that happen, until—" She cleared her throat. "Until he was killed by a bank robber."

"I'm sorry."

"Yes, me too. But it does give me some comfort to know he didn't suffer long."

"Was anyone else hurt in the robbery?" Jesse asked in spite of the fact that he knew his curiosity teetered on the verge of being morbid.

"I wasn't there, of course, so everything I know came from other people … but I heard that he died trying to save everyone else."

Jesse thought for a moment so he wouldn't say the wrong

thing. "That was a very honorable thing for him to do."

"I know, but it still hurts." She grew silent for a moment before turning to him. "And how about you?"

"I gather now you want to talk about the family I lost." His chest constricted at the very thought of discussing his wife and children who had been so precious to him.

"Only if you can."

He sucked in a deep breath and slowly blew it out. Since he'd already asked her about her husband, and she answered without hesitation, he figured she deserved the same treatment.

"I had just left the house to see a new baby who wasn't expected to live more than a few hours. They sent someone for me so I could be with the family to console them when he took his last breath." Jesse stopped for a few seconds to gather his thoughts. "We aren't positive exactly what happened, but we think that an escaped ember from the fireplace must have caused it. It happened at about the time Viola would have been putting our children to bed. They were unable to get out of the house in time."

Lenora reached out and placed her hand on his. "I am so sorry that happened to you and your family. It just goes to show that we must be ready for the Lord at all times."

He was surprised by how comforting her gentle touch and Christ-centered words were. For the first time since the fire, he felt an odd sense of peace.

Chapter 6

Lenora sensed an immediate change in Pastor Grant. She didn't intend to touch him, but her instinctive act garnered a look from him that said more than words ever could. She felt a tug at her heart that surprised her.

"We are almost there," he said, his tone much lighter. "I almost forgot to ask. What is in that basket?"

"Some muffins that Julia and I made from a recipe our mother used."

"I have always liked muffins." Jesse smiled at her, and this time she could see a flicker of humor.

"If that's a hint, I would be happy to sneak one or two out of the basket for you to take home later." She grinned back at him. As their gazes locked, a strange sensation fluttered in her abdomen.

"I would like that very much."

He turned his attention back to steering the horse down the road as she pulled out a napkin, wrapped a couple of the muffins, and set them aside. "There are still plenty for Pastor and Mrs. Ledbetter."

"They can only eat so many muffins."

The sound of his laughter that followed lifted her spirits

considerably. She took another long look at Jesse and saw that behind his gruff exterior was a man with heart and humor. She found that very attractive.

The pastor and his wife greeted them at the door. Mrs. Ledbetter took the basket from her. "You really didn't have to do this, but I certainly appreciate it. We're just happy that you went to the trouble of coming this long way just to have supper with us."

For the next several hours, Lenora had the most fun she'd had since Harvey had died. She could tell that Jesse was enjoying himself as well. And when she saw the way the pastor and his wife looked at each other, she was well aware that they had noticed.

After supper, Mrs. Ledbetter asked her to join her in the kitchen. "You don't have to lift a finger, but I would love some company while I do the dishes."

"Nonsense." Lenora picked up a towel. "I insist on helping. It is the least I can do. Besides, work is always more fun when you do it with someone you enjoy being around."

Mrs. Ledbetter smiled at her. "You are so right. I'll wash, and you can dry."

They made small talk until they put away the last plate. Then Mrs. Ledbetter turned around to face her but didn't say anything right away.

Lenora tilted her head. "Why do I get the feeling you're about to tell me something important?"

"It is not what I'm about to tell you but a question I need to ask."

"And that is …?"

"Have you thought about whether or not you want to marry Jesse?" Mrs. Ledbetter took Lenora's hands in hers. "You don't have to answer me, but you'll need to make a decision fairly soon."

"I have thought about it." Lenora left out the fact that until that afternoon, her answer would have been no. "It is something that Pastor … I mean Jesse and I will have to

DEBBY MAYNE

discuss. I'm not sure he is ready to get married again."

"Well, in case it has any bearing on your decision, I want you to know that I have seen something different in him since the two of you have been here today."

Lenora nodded. "Yes, I noticed it on the way here. We had a chance to talk, and I think it might have helped."

"Talking is always good. And since both of you know the ultimate source of grace, it is especially helpful if you ever hope to have a relationship."

They chatted for a few more minutes before Jesse came to the kitchen door. "We need to head on back, Lenora. As it is, it will be dark before I have you home."

After they said their goodbyes to the Ledbetters, they went to the carriage. She started to get in, but he stopped her. "Let me help you up."

He took her hand and gave her a boost. Once she was settled in her seat, he went around to the other side and got in. That very simple act spoke volumes and confirmed that something had definitely changed between them.

All the way to Julia's house, they chatted about the wonderful time they had that evening. When they finally arrived, he helped her out. "Would you mind if I call on you tomorrow?"

She nodded. "That would be good."

*

The next afternoon, he arrived shortly after the noon meal. Julia offered to take Andrew outside to play, but Jesse insisted on having him stay.

"I have a surprise for Andrew," Jesse said.

Julia lifted her eyebrows and shot Lenora a glance of satisfaction before turning back to Jesse. "In that case, I will go out back with my children. I would never want to deprive my nephew of any surprises." She went to the door. "I will tell Andrew that you want to see him."

A few minutes later, Andrew arrived. "What did you want me for, Mama?" he asked.

Lenora tipped her head toward Jesse. "Pastor Grant has a surprise for you."

Andrew's eyebrows shot up. "A surprise?"

Jesse stood up and pulled something from his pocket. "Have you ever played with a top, Andrew?"

Lenora's heart melted as Jesse showed her son how to spin the top. "Wherever did you get that?" she asked.

"I carved it last night. I thought he might enjoy something new to play with."

"May I try?" Andrew asked.

"Yes, of course." Jesse handed Andrew the top. After a few futile attempts to get it to spin, Jesse leaned over. "Want me to show you how?"

Over the next half hour, Lenora watched in amazement as this once churlish man showed patience and kindness toward her son. He was quickly winning her heart. His time to leave came much too quickly, and Lenora was sad to see him go.

"Would you like to join me the day after tomorrow? I have to go to town, and while we are there, maybe we can get something from the grocer and go on a picnic?"

"A picnic?" Andrew said as he hopped around. "I love picnics."

Lenora tightened her lips and gave Jesse a sideways glance. She wasn't sure if Jesse intended to take Andrew, but now that her little boy knew about it, she sure did hope so.

"Good! So do I." Jesse smiled at Lenora. "I think this will be delightful, just the three of us spending the day together in Golden."

*

Jesse couldn't figure out why he was so nervous about taking Lenora and her boy to town. He'd already decided that he liked both of them, and he thought Lenora would make a fine wife. Now all he needed to do was court her and show her that he wasn't always as petulant as he was when they first met.

Andrew came running out as soon as Jesse turned down

the dirt road leading to Julia and Stone's house. Jesse stopped the carriage and let the boy get in before pulling all the way up to the porch, where Lenora stood waiting.

She gave him an apologetic look. "I tried to stop him, but he took off too quickly when he saw you coming. You've definitely won him over."

"That's okay. I'm actually flattered that he was so happy to see me coming." And he was. It had been a long time since anyone had shown this much enthusiasm merely by his presence.

Throughout the morning, Jesse got to know Lenora. He learned that she was very family minded, enjoyed cooking and sewing, but didn't care much for large crowds. He shared with her that socializing with the entire church body had been one of the most difficult things for him as well, but it was something that came with his job as pastor.

"Do you like being a pastor?" she asked.

"Other than having to mill about during potluck events, I like everything about it." He stopped and turned her around to face him while Andrew watched one of the shoe cobblers through the store window. "Now how about you? Do you think you would like being the wife of a pastor?"

She blinked before slowly nodding. "Yes, I think I would like it very much."

His heart hammered. When he'd first been told he needed to find a wife, he doubted he would ever feel right about it, even though he was willing to at least consider whatever was needed to satisfy the church leaders. But now that he'd gotten to know Lenora and her little boy, his thoughts were different. But he still wanted to give it some more time.

"Perhaps after church tomorrow, you can stay behind, and we can talk some more," he said softly.

"I'll have to ask my sister if she minds taking Andrew."

"He can stay too." Jesse preferred having Lenora to himself, but if Julia wasn't able to take Andrew, he would accept that.

"Let me talk to Julia first."

Jesse let Andrew pick out what he wanted for his picnic from the grocer and meat market. Both Jesse and Lenora laughed at the immense amount of food he wanted.

"You can't have that much food, Andrew," Lenora said. "Pick one or two things."

"But Mama ..." Andrew frowned and then slowly nodded. "Okay, I would like the sausage and apple."

Jesse pulled Lenora aside. "I really don't mind if he wants more. I can take it home and have what is left for supper."

"Are you sure?" The concern on his face let him know that she was sincere.

He nodded. "Yes, in fact, I insist. Let him pick out anything he wants."

Andrew was ecstatic. In addition to the sausage and apples, he chose cheese, cookies, and carrots. Jesse belted out a hearty chuckle, and soon Lenora and Andrew laughed right along with him.

On their way back to the carriage, Jesse pointed to a general store. "I need to run in here real quick. Why don't you and Andrew wait here for me?"

He knew about a clearing in the forest on the way back to Julia and Stone's house. "Ooh, this is lovely." Lenora took a long look around. "What a beautiful spot for a picnic."

Once again, Jesse reached into his pocket and pulled out a surprise. This time it was bubbles. "This is what I purchased at the store. I thought Andrew might like it."

"I love bubbles!" Andrew said.

"Would you like to blow them or have me blow them and you chase them?" Jesse asked.

"I can chase them!"

Jesse pulled out the bubble wand and started blowing, sending bubbles through the air over the grassy field. Lenora stood and watched, a smile of satisfaction covering her pretty face.

Epilogue

(Four weeks later)

"Why are you so nervous, Lenora?" Julia asked as she stood watching Lenora brush her hair. "It's not like you have never been on a picnic with Jesse before."

"I know, but this seems different." Lenora stopped brushing her hair and turned to face her sister. "I think he might ask me to marry him."

Julia tilted her head. "Isn't that why you came here in the first place?"

"Yes, but I didn't expect any romance." She resumed brushing her hair. "I saw it more as a marriage of convenience—for him to have a wife to help with his ministry and for me to have someone to take care of Andrew and me."

"But you've fallen in love." Julia smiled. "That is definitely a bonus."

Lenora stood up and turned around to face her sister. "It is so hard to believe. I never thought it would actually happen. I assumed that Harvey would be the only man I could love."

"The Lord had different ideas, though, so here you are." Julia put her arms out to her sides, palms up.

"Yes, here I am." She took a deep breath. "Do I look presentable?"

"For a picnic?" Julia laughed. "Oh, that's right. You think he might propose." She made a face. "What if he doesn't?"

"He sort of already did." Lenora gave her sister a sheepish look. "Simply by sending for me to be his mail order bride, I suppose it was assumed ..."

"Remember what you said about the romance," Julia said. "Don't try to take the romance out of it."

"Oh, trust me, I'm not. In fact, look at you." Lenora gave her a sideways look. "You were a mail order bride, and your marriage appears to be very romantic."

"It is, isn't it?"

They both laughed. Finally, Lenora pulled herself together, took one last look in the mirror, and spun around to face Julia. "You never answered my question. Do I look presentable?"

"You, my sweet sister, look more than presentable. You absolutely glow with beauty—the kind that only comes from loving and being loved."

Lenora rolled her eyes and chuckled. "I will take that as a yes."

There was a knock on the bedroom door followed by Stone's voice. "Pastor Grant is here."

"Please tell him I will be there in a moment."

"Don't make him wait too long." Stone laughed as he walked back to toward the front of the house.

Julia placed her hands on Lenora's shoulders and looked her in the eye. "You look positively beautiful. Now go to Pastor Grant or Jesse or whatever he wants to be called."

"Yes, ma'am."

As soon as Lenora walked into the front room, her heart hammered at the sight of Jesse Grant. The warmth of his smile combined with his masculine demeanor and larger-than-life frame gave her the feeling of protection.

"Are you ready for a picnic, Lenora?"

She smiled back at him. "I absolutely am."

"Then let's go."

As he drove the carriage past Stone and Julia's property, all of her senses were on heightened alert. The birds sang louder than ever, the sky was bluer than blue, and the fragrance of grass, trees, and wildflowers filled her nostrils. He barely got past the first patch of forest when he pulled off to the side of the road.

She looked at him with trepidation. "Is something wrong, Jesse?"

"Yes." He forced a frown, but he didn't quite hide the smile that teased the corners of his lips. He got out of the carriage, came around to her side, and lifted her out without a muscle twitching. "Before we go another inch, there is something I have to ask."

"My answer is yes."

He tilted his head back and roared with laughter before looking back down into her eyes. "At least let me get the question out before you give me an answer."

"Okay." She straightened her shoulders and lifted her chin. "Ask the question please."

"Will you--?"

"Yes." She lifted her fingertips to her lips. "Oops. Sorry."

Again, he laughed. "Let me try this one more time."

"Okay, I'll try to behave."

"Lenora, will you please do me the honor of ..." He tilted his head toward her and teased her with a long pause.

"Come on, Jesse. Don't do this to me."

"Lenora, I would love nothing more than to have you marry me. I want to be your husband and Andrew's father. Will you be my wife?"

She threw her arms around his neck and hugged him with all her might. He finally peeled her arms away and looked her in the eyes.

"Well? Will you?"

"Of course I will."

He hugged her and then lifted her back into the carriage. "Now we can relax and enjoy our picnic."

"Andrew will be delighted," Lenora said as they rode to their destination.

"I hope he's not the only one."

"Oh, trust me, he isn't." She leaned into him and looked up at his bearded face. "We will have a wonderful life together."

"Yes, I know that." Jesse pulled over again, put his arms around Lenora, and kissed her. "And we just might add another child or two. You are such a wonderful mother, it would be a shame not to."

"I have one question, though," she said. "What do you want Andrew to call you?"

Jesse shrugged. "I don't suppose it really matters ..." He smiled at her. "As long as it's Papa or Daddy." He leaned down and gave her a kiss on the forehead. "And you may call me sweetheart."

Mary's Improbable Marriage

Hollister Sisters Mail Order Brides

Debby Mayne

Husbands, love your wives, even as Christ also loved the
church, and gave himself for it ...

Ephesians 5:25

Chapter 1

(May 1884, Virginia)

Mary lifted her head off the pillow at the sound of someone rapping on her bedroom door. She cleared her throat as she sat up and took a long look around in the semi-darkness. It was awfully early. Maybe she'd dreamed the sound.

But then it happened again, only this time louder and with more urgency. She stood and slipped into the robe she'd hung on the footboard post as she padded across the massive room toward the door. The household supervisor was on the other side, appearing staid as always.

Mary smiled, in spite of the fact that she knew it wouldn't be returned. "Did you need me for something?"

"Yes. The lady of the house has asked me to inform you that your services will no longer be needed."

"What?" Mary squinted at the woman whose expression didn't change. "My services are no longer needed? Are you telling me that I've been ... fired?"

"You may call it whatever you like, but you have until noon to pack your bags and leave."

"But—"

The woman turned her back and left Mary standing there staring after her. After she realized her mouth was hanging open, she closed it, backed into the room that had been hers for the past several years, and closed the door. Only then did she allow the tears to fall.

She should have listened to the children. The oldest one had mentioned that her aunt—her mother's newly widowed aunt—might come to live with them, and if that happened, Mary might not be needed. But the children were all practical jokers, so she assumed that was all it was—a joke.

Fortunately, she didn't have much to pack. Her employer had provided her with uniforms, so all she had in the closet that belonged to her were a couple of outfits she wore to church and to visit her family. Then it dawned on her. The only place she could go was back home, and that would be awful, considering what a difficult time Papa had been having lately.

Mary knew that he had sent Julia and Lenora to Colorado to marry men they didn't even know because he could no longer afford to feed them. Fortunately for them, they were happy in their new homes, but she couldn't expect to be allowed to stay in the old family home for free … at least not for long. She knew Papa wouldn't turn her away, but she would need to find some way to support herself.

Of the four sisters, Mary knew she was the least attractive with mousy brown hair and hazel eyes that were set a bit too far apart. But she was smart. She knew how to cook, sew, and clean. And children typically adored her because she was quick with a joke and didn't mind playing games as long as they showed respect. Maybe she'd be able to get another job taking care of children.

She changed out of her nightclothes and into a dress. Then she stuffed all of her personal belongings into the trunk she'd arrived with. Surely, she'd be able to get Henry to help her home. He'd been with the Schofield family since long before she arrived and he'd always been very kind.

After she shut the trunk, she ventured out into the hall. The sound of Mrs. Schofield's shoes coming toward her made her turn around.

"Hi, Mary. I'm sorry for such short notice, but my aunt will be here tomorrow evening, and we have to get your room ready for her." She pulled an envelope from her skirt pocket and held it out to Mary. "This is for you. It's a little bit of money that should help you until you find another position."

Mary looked at it, wishing she could turn it down, before accepting it. "Thank you." The words came out so quietly she wasn't sure Mrs. Schofield could hear.

"Is there anything else?" Mrs. Schofield asked.

"Yes, ma'am. Can Henry … or someone help me with this trunk?"

"Oh. Of course. Where are you going?"

"Home, I suppose." Mary swallowed hard. This was one of the most difficult situations she'd ever been in.

"That's in town, right?"

"Yes, ma'am."

"Let me go see if Henry can take you. If not, I'm sure there will be someone who can."

Before Mary had a chance to say another word, Mrs. Schofield took off down the hall and disappeared around the corner. Mary remained standing there, wondering what the future held for her.

*

(Golden, Colorado)

Lester Packard stared at the charred remains of the house he'd been living in since he'd arrived in Golden, Colorado. It hadn't been much of a house—built in a hurry since he knew no one and had no place to stay when he'd first arrived. He'd come for the gold, hoping to strike it rich, but in the meantime, he had to have a place to stay. He now had money from the gold, but the house was not salvageable.

For the past three years, all he'd done was work. He still went to the gold mines nearly every day, but he also tended his land that he'd purchased from Stone Michaels. Weary from all the hard work, he barely had the energy to drag himself into bed each night, so he hadn't done anything to improve his living conditions. Now he had no choice.

The sound of a horse's hooves came from behind. When he turned around, he spotted Stone coming toward him.

"What happened?"

Lester shook his head. "I forgot to put out the fire before I left this morning, and I came home to this."

"Looks like nothing's left." Stone leaned back on his horse. "Tell you what, Lester. Why don't you come on over to my place. We have plenty of room."

"I would rather not." Lester glanced at the remains before casting his gaze downward.

"What other choice do you have? You can't very well sleep on the ground without any blankets."

Stone was right. Lester didn't have any other choice. Finally, he blew out a breath he'd been holding and nodded.

"Okay, I'll stay at your place but only until I find something else for myself."

Stone let out a sympathetic chuckle. "I hope you're not counting on the hotel in town. They haven't had a vacant room in as long as I can remember, with all the men coming to strike it rich."

"I'll think of something."

"I would tell you to get your things, but from the looks of this, you don't have any things to get." Stone pointed to the barn. "Are your horses in there?"

"Yeah, I'll saddle up and be at your place when I get there."

"Don't take too long. Julia's cooking up a big pot of stew." Stone grinned. "My wife makes the best beef stew in all of Colorado."

Lester's mouth watered. He couldn't remember the last time he'd had a decent meal. He'd been subsisting on beans and whatever folks from the church brought over. It was mostly pies, so he wasn't about to complain, but a bowl of beef stew sure did sound delicious.

Stone turned his horse away from Lester before glancing over his shoulder. "I'll tell Julia to set another place. See you in a little while."

Before Lester could put up another argument, Stone took off, leaving Lester standing there wondering what to do next. He didn't want to overstay his welcome at Stone's house. Maybe he'd think more clearly after eating some stew.

He went to the barn, saddled up his favorite horse, and headed in the direction of Stone's large house. Lester had always thought he'd have something just as nice, but as time went on, he didn't see any reason to have anything else built. It was just him, and what did he need with a large, rambling ranch house?

Lester's family back East had thought he was crazy to come to Colorado. They'd begged him to stay and marry his father's best friend's daughter. But he wasn't ready to settle down back then. Folks said he had bugs in his britches, but he knew he simply wasn't ready for a wife and everything that came with having one.

He'd only recently started thinking he might like a wife, but he knew he was probably too set in his ways to attract the kind of woman he'd want. Besides, there were so few women in these parts that men resorted to sending off for mail order brides.

That was what Stone had done, and it had turned out just fine for him. But Lester doubted he'd be so lucky. The pastor had said luck had nothing to do with it, which gave him all the more reason not to do that. Lester was fully aware that people called him a grouch behind his back ... and rightfully so. He couldn't remember the last time he'd smiled.

Stone stood on the front porch of his house, waiting for

him. As soon as he dismounted his horse, Stone gestured toward the door.

"We've already got a place set for you. Julia is feeding the children now, and then the adults will eat."

"Don't you eat with your kids?" Lester asked.

"Most of the time we do, but when we have special company ..." Stone grinned. "We thought it might be nice to have some adult conversation."

Lester hoped he wouldn't have to wait long before chowing down. Now that he could smell the stew cooking, his stomach was starting to rumble.

Fortunately for him, Julia's efficiency was in full force. The children were finishing their dinner, and the oldest one had been given the task of helping the younger ones get ready for bed.

"I'm terribly sorry to hear about your place, Lester," Julia said as she turned back to the stove where the pot of stew was simmering.

He shrugged. "It wasn't much of a place."

Stone patted him on the shoulder. "We'll get a bunch of men from the church to help you build something nicer."

Lester caught Stone exchanging a glance with Julia. It appeared that there was more to the look than met the eye, but Lester wasn't about to pry. Not that he'd ever find out firsthand, but he knew husbands and wives communicated in odd ways.

A few minutes later, they sat down at the table, big bowls heaping with stew filled with meat, potatoes, onions, and carrots in front of them. Lester started to pick up his spoon, but Stone bowed his head and started praying, so he followed suit.

When they opened their eyes, Julia grinned. "Would you like to know what we've been thinking?"

"Julia!" Stone gave her a teasing look. "This conversation was supposed to wait until later."

"I can't wait." Julia turned back to Lester, and before he

DEBBY MAYNE

had a chance to say a word, she continued. "You already know that I came here as a mail order bride. Well ..." She grinned at her husband and turned back to Lester. "There is a long list of women who are willing and even eager to move here."

Lester swallowed a bite of stew. "What are you saying?"

Stone looked at Julia and shook his head. "I'm afraid he's not used to this kind of indirect talk. You need to give it to him straight." He turned his gaze toward Lester. "You need a wife. We've been thinking that for quite a while now, and what happened only proves it. If someone had been home, that fire never would have happened."

"I don't need a wife." As soon as those words escaped Lester's mouth, he knew there was no conviction in his voice. "I can get along just fine without one."

"You're not getting any younger," Stone reminded him. "And if you ever want to have a family of your own—"

"I've never been one of those men who always wanted a family." In fact, there were times he thought he was just as well off without one.

"We understand that, Lester," Julia said in a calm tone. "But you don't sound happy most of the time."

Lester glanced down at his stew before meeting her gaze again. "A man doesn't always have to be happy."

She smiled. "I think your unhappiness is the result of not having anyone at home to keep you company."

"I don't know." Lester cleared his throat before eating more of his stew. "This sure is good, Julia."

She glanced over at her husband before looking back at Lester. "If you have a wife, you might have something this good or better waiting for you every single night."

Now that she put it that way ...

*

A month later, Mary stood with Sarah as they watched Papa approach the house after work.

"Uh oh." Sarah made a face. "I know that look."

102

"What look?" Mary squinted her eyes and saw an expression she'd never seen on Papa's face.

"He's at it again." Sarah's shoulder's slumped as she turned away from the window. "One of us is about to be sent away to get married off."

"That's just plain ridiculous," Mary said.

"Mark my words. You'll see."

Mary tilted her head as Papa walked inside, a silly grin on his face. "As soon as I get cleaned up, I need to talk to you girls. What's for supper?"

Sarah looked at Mary, who spoke up. "Meatloaf."

"Perfect. I'll be out in a few minutes."

Sarah followed Mary over to the kitchen area and helped put out some dishes. "See? He's getting ready to send one of us away." She shuddered. "One of us is about to become a mail order bride."

Mary laughed. "It won't be me. No one would pick me out of a catalog."

"Oh, it's not just from a catalog. Papa has been communicating with some of the pastors in Golden, Colorado."

"That's where Julia and Lenora are, right?"

Sarah nodded. "I sure would love to see them again, but not if I have to marry some old, ugly rancher."

"I doubt either of them would have married an old, ugly rancher," Mary said as she carried the plates of meatloaf and mashed potatoes to the table.

"I don't know." Sarah's attention turned to Papa who had come up from behind Mary.

"Let's say the blessing, girls. I can't wait to tell you what's going on." He pulled up a chair and plopped down. "I'm starving."

A few minutes later, all three of them sat at the table in silence—with Papa shoveling food into his mouth as fast as he could. Mary tried to eat, but Papa's demeanor caused a knot to form in the pit of her stomach. She glanced at Sarah's plate and saw that she'd lost her appetite.

"What did you want to discuss?" Mary finally asked.

He put down his fork and leaned back in his chair, his gaze going back and forth between his daughters. "I know you might not understand—or like—this, but it isn't something I can change. There isn't enough money coming in for all of us to stay here."

"But I gave you some money when I came back home," Mary argued. "In fact, I only kept one dollar from the cash Mrs. Schofield gave me when she let me go."

"Yes, I'm aware of that." Papa forced a smile. "And I certainly appreciate your willingness to contribute. But the fact remains, that money won't last forever. A month, maybe, but after that—" He sighed and shook his head. "I don't know what we'll do."

"I'll get another job," Mary offered.

"Doing what?" Papa shook his head. "There is nothing for you girls here anyway. Most of the good men are married … or they've gone west. I think it's time …" His voice trailed off as Sarah stood up and ran to her room. "Why is she acting like that? It's not like I can help it."

Mary smiled and covered her father's hand with hers. "She is upset that you're sending her away. I'm sure she'll come around."

"I'm not sending her." Papa leveled her with one of his steely gazes. "You are the one this man wants."

Mary's chin dropped, and her eyes widened. "Me? But why?"

Chapter 2

He shrugged. "Apparently, he is more interested in a woman who is capable of doing all of the things around the house than having a pretty face waiting for him when he comes in after a long day's work."

"No, I'm afraid I can't do it."

"Mary ..." The weariness in his eyes broke Mary's heart. "Believe me when I say that if there was anything I could do to change things, I would. But it's too late for me. All I can hope for is to find suitable husbands for all of my daughters—men who are willing to take care of you and make sure you have a nice home and plenty of food to eat."

"But I have never imagined myself getting married." She had always been the least probable of all the Hollister sisters to ever marry ... at least in her thoughts.

"This isn't something any of us imagined happening." Papa's voice shook. "The probability of any woman finding a good husband here is slim. There just aren't enough kind and caring men to go around."

"How do you know the men out west are kind and caring?"

He glanced down and then slowly raised his pained gaze.

"I didn't know for certain when I sent Julia, but Stone said she could stay with his pastor before the wedding and if she decided not to go through with it, he would send her home."

"What do you know about this man that you want me to marry?"

"Julia seems to like him. She thinks he is a kind man who will make a good husband and father."

The tone of his voice touched Mary more than his words. She could tell that he didn't want to send any of his daughters away and this was a last resort. How could she simply say no to a man who had done so much for her and looked like his entire world had caved in around him.

"Okay, if this is the only way, I'll go." She willed herself not to cry. "I know you want what is best for us."

He nodded. "I always have."

"Yes, and perhaps this is the best thing for me." She stood up and carried her half-empty plate to the counter before turning to Papa and forcing a smile. "I just hope he doesn't run away screaming when he sees me."

Papa stood up and closed the distance between them. "You might not have the same classic beauty of your sisters, but to me, you are just as pretty. You have a heart of gold, and you have never let anyone down." He took her hand and squeezed it. "Look at you. Even now, you're doing something in the best interest of the family."

Mary gave her father a quick hug. "I need to go let Sarah know. She is completely distraught over the very notion of being a mail order bride."

"I know. What I don't understand is why none of the men I've communicated with are interested in her." Papa frowned. "She is such a pretty girl."

"As you said, there is more to being pretty than looks."

*

Six weeks later, Lester shifted his weight from one foot to the other beside the railroad, waiting for his new bride-to-be. Stone and Julia had offered to come to the train station with him, but he preferred meeting Mary alone, without anyone's judging eyes.

The sound of the approaching train caused his pulse to quicken, and now he found himself doubting why he'd ever done such a thing as to ask to marry a woman he had never met. Sure, he knew that Mary was Julia's sister, but he'd seen how different people in the same family could be. His own siblings were a testament to that.

A couple of men stepped off the train, followed by a woman with several children. Then he spotted her. She looked exactly like her picture—attractive but not pretty in the traditional sense. But someone he would enjoy looking at from across the table.

When their gazes met, she gave him a questioning look. He nodded and smiled as he walked toward her.

"Mary?" he asked.

Her smile widened, but her lips quivered. He found comfort in knowing that she was as nervous as he was. "You must be Lester."

"Yes." He looked around. "Let's get your things and put them in the carriage. The pastor is waiting for us."

Mary licked her lips and then pursed them. Now he wasn't sure about all the plans he'd made.

"Did your father tell you that we are getting married on the way to the house?"

She nodded. "Yes."

"If you don't want to ... I mean, that is, if—"

Mary lifted her chin. "That is what I came here for, and it's what I'll do."

The look on her face wasn't anything like what he'd hoped to see on his bride. She didn't appear fazed by his attempt at kindness—something that didn't come natural to him anymore. He'd been alone for so long that he'd forgotten how to make small talk. The only time he typically saw people was on Sundays at church. And he made it a point to say as little as possible and get away as quickly as he could without creating a stir.

He gathered her belongings and hoisted them into the carriage. He was surprised by how little she'd brought. Julia had told him that Mary was a minimalist, but he still expected more than this.

She clearly didn't want to make conversation, which was just fine by him. He took the reins and guided the carriage toward Pastor Ledbetter's house. Stone said Julia had begged to be there, but Lester had made it very clear that he didn't want too much fuss made over the wedding.

After a half hour, Mary turned to him, and without smiling, struck up a conversation. "How much land do you have?"

"About fifty acres. Some of it is too hilly to farm or use for cattle, but I have enough to get by."

"That's good to know." She looked around. "How much farther to the pastor's house?"

"We should be there in about fifteen minutes." He kept his tone as even as possible. Several people from the church had jumped when he spoke, so he knew he could sound harsh.

"Is there a store nearby where I can purchase essentials?"

"The town of Golden has pretty much anything you might need."

She nodded. He allowed himself to look at her for several seconds, hoping to see some sign of emotion. But no, all he saw was a woman who was resigned to coming to Colorado because her father could no longer provide for her.

If Lester were any younger, he might try to find a way to make her love him, but those days were long gone. All he wanted was to get through life without being a burden on anyone. Taking a wife was part of his means to do that. He would spend his days in the gold mines and on the ranch, while she took care of everything in the home. And he'd have a decent meal around the time the sun went down each evening. What more could someone like him expect? He wasn't exactly the most desirable man around, and he certainly didn't have the charm that drew women.

When Lester took the final turn toward the pastor's house, he saw Mary's entire body tense. He had a feeling she was frightened of him, although it was obvious that she didn't want him to know that.

"You will have your own room when we get to my house—I mean our home ... at least until you are ready to come to my room."

She quickly turned around to face him, a hint of relief showing on her face. "Is that all right with you?"

He shrugged. "I don't know that it matters whether or not it's all right with me. If that is what you want, then that is what you should have. No woman should be forced to do anything she doesn't want to do."

The muscles in her shoulders seemed to relax a bit. "Thank you, Mr. Packard."

"Lester." He cast a smile in her direction. "You must call me Lester. That is, unless you want me to call you Mrs. Packard."

She gave him a comical look as the corners of her lips tilted up. "Okay, I'll call you Lester."

At least some of her distress had faded. "Regardless of what we call each other, we will be husband and wife."

*

A few minutes later, Mary's legs wobbled as she realized what she had just done. Saying her vows to this man she'd met only an hour ago wasn't something she had dreamed about all her life, but it was real.

"You are now husband and wife," Pastor Ledbetter said. He turned to his wife. "Is the coffee ready?"

Mrs. Ledbetter offered a warm smile as she nodded. "Yes, but I would like to have a few words with Mary before we have refreshments."

Mary glanced at Lester who nodded. She followed Mrs. Ledbetter to another room in the parsonage.

"Please have a seat, Mary." The older woman gestured toward a chair. As soon as Mary sat down, Mrs. Ledbetter chose a chair adjacent to hers. "I understand that you have cared for other people's children for several years."

Mary smiled at the kind woman who was clearly trying to put her at ease. "Yes, ma'am."

"That experience will serve you well later, although I suspect it will be a little bit different with your own children."

An odd sensation flooded Mary. Having her own children wasn't something Mary had ever considered for more than a fleeting moment.

"But that might not be soon ... or ever," Mrs. Ledbetter continued. "In the meantime, there will be plenty for you to do on the ranch. And we have some wonderful activities at the church." She paused and smiled. "Do you like to cook?"

"Sometimes. Julia and Lenora did most of the cooking when we were younger, but I can make do in the kitchen."

"If you ever need any help, I am sure your sisters will be happy to assist. And you can always count on me for whatever they can't do."

"Thank you." Mary cast her gaze downward. She liked Mrs. Ledbetter, but she didn't want to appear too needy. "I am sure I'll be fine, though."

Mrs. Ledbetter's expression grew more serious. "Have you seen Lester's ... I mean your house?"

"Not yet. We came straight here."

Mrs. Ledbetter grew quiet for a moment before looking directly at Mary again. "Did he tell you anything about the house?"

"All I know is that it burned down and had to be rebuilt."

"That is true. The new house is finished, but the furnishings are sparse."

Mary nodded. "I am fine with that." She remembered Lester mentioning that she would have her own room ... at least at first. "I have never had much of my own, so I am easy to please."

The older woman gave her a serene smile. "None of it belongs to us anyway. It is all His."

"Yes, I know." Mary broke their gaze. She didn't want Mrs. Ledbetter to see her shame from not having attended church as often as she should have.

"What is wrong, Mary?" Mrs. Ledbetter's tone was filled with compassion.

Mary's eyes filled with tears, and there was nothing she could do to stop them. She sniffled and did her best to avoid the older woman's gaze.

"Oh dear, I've made you cry."

Mary shook her head. "You didn't make me cry. I'm just so …"

"Overwhelmed?"

Mary nodded. "Yes, that's what I'm feeling right now. I never thought I would marry, and I certainly never thought I'd move to Colorado."

"But why?"

"It's so far away from what I know."

Mrs. Ledbetter chuckled. "What I'm asking is why you never thought you would marry."

Mary smiled through the tears. "Look at me. I am not exactly what anyone would call a pretty girl."

"I think you are very attractive." Mrs. Ledbetter paused. "You are at least as pretty as I ever was, and I have been married for quite a while. Having a pretty face is not required for love, you know."

"That's another thing. I didn't marry for love."

"Lester Packard is a good man." The older woman squeezed Mary's hand again before letting go. "He just needs a little bit of refinement—something that will come over time, after the two of you grow used to each other."

"Are you saying I should try to change him?"

"No, of course not. A wife's job is never to change her husband but to show him how to love and be loved. And that will come naturally as you spend more time together."

The sound of men's voices coming closer caught their attention. Mary looked up in time to see the pastor appear at the door. "We should have our refreshments now so Lester can take his new bride home."

The next half hour was filled with coffee, food, and conversation. When Mary stood up to help Mrs. Ledbetter, the older woman gestured toward the door. "I can take care of this by myself. Lester is waiting for you." She gave Mary a hug. "I will pray for you."

"Thank you." Mary swallowed hard. "I appreciate everything."

Lester gave her a look of impatience before turning around and heading toward the door. She didn't hesitate to go after him.

As soon as they were on their way, Lester started talking. "I want to warn you, the house is bare."

"I understand." Mary imagined bare walls and possibly a dirt floor with a kitchen that had very little to work with. "I don't need anything fancy."

He tossed a curious look at her. "You are a most unusual woman, Mary. I think we will get along just fine."

They passed several other ranches with homes of various sizes and shapes. When he turned onto a small dirt road, his mood changed, so her pulse quickened.

"This is my property," Lester said in a monotone. "The house is just around that patch of trees."

As soon as the house came into view, Mary blinked. "That is your house?"

"Yes." He lifted one eyebrow as he turned to her. "I hope you are not terribly disappointed."

Mary was momentarily speechless. The house was much larger than the one she'd grown up in. The outside of it was rough-cut lumber, but she could tell that Lester was a man of more means than she initially realized.

"Are you rich?" As soon as the words left her mouth, she

wanted to crawl under the carriage.

He let out a booming laugh. "I have money, yes, but that is not what makes a man rich."

"I didn't mean—"

"I know what you meant." He pointed to the house. "The house that burned was much smaller than this one. I decided that since you were coming, it would be a good idea to build something that could accommodate a family." He tilted his head toward her and looked at her from beneath his heavy eyebrows. "A very large family."

Mary instantly went numb. He couldn't have stunned her more if he'd knocked her over the head with a club.

"I would like to start having children within the next year, but for now, I will be content with finishing my ... our home. I left quite a bit unfinished since I figured you would want some say in things."

"Um ..." She cleared her throat. "That was very nice of you."

"I want my wife to be happy, and since this is your home too, it is only right."

"Thank you."

They came to a stop directly in front of the house. The front porch was wide and deep, providing ample space for rocking chairs and a table. She had always liked porches—something her father's house never had.

"Let's go inside before I bring your things in."

She nodded and allowed him to help her down from the carriage. As they walked through the house, she continued to be surprised by the many different things she hadn't expected. First of all, there was a wood floor, and the front room had furniture. It was still sparse, but she didn't expect this much.

They went to the kitchen next. "It already has a stove," she said.

"Of course. I couldn't very well expect you to cook over an open fire. If you need anything else, I will get it for you."

He walked over to an open doorway. "This is the pantry. I haven't had much success with gardening, but I thought you could do that. If you don't know how, the pastor's wife will teach you. She said she would also show you how to can vegetables."

"I can already do that." Mary was thankful for the time she'd spent with the Schofields' cook while the children were sleeping.

"Now I will show you to your room." Without another word, he led her down a long hallway, past several empty bedrooms, to the room at the very end. He gestured toward the door. "This is where you will stay until you decide you want to join me in my room. I'm sorry the room is so small."

As she walked into the room, she was speechless. Never in her life had she had such a beautiful space of her own— not even at the Schofield mansion. In the center of the room was a large bed with a wrought iron headboard and footboard. The bed was made up with a quilt and eyelet-trimmed pillowcases. A dresser that had many more drawers than she would ever need stood beside a small vanity with a cushioned stool. On the adjacent wall was a wardrobe.

"I wasn't sure what you would need," he said softly.

"This is wonderful." Mary looked around the room several times before turning back to Lester. "You didn't have to go to all of this trouble."

"That was what I thought, but your sister insisted on getting this room ready."

"Which sister?" Mary asked.

"Julia. She and Stone brought everything over, and she spent a couple of hours making sure everything was just right."

He scowled as he spoke, so Mary wasn't sure what he was thinking. "Did I do something wrong?"

"No." His demeanor had changed, and he was back to his grouchy self. "Stay here while I go get your things."

"I can help." She started after him.

He stopped and turned around to face her. "I told you to stay here."

His commanding tone made her cringe. "Okay."

The second he left her alone, she walked over and opened the wardrobe. The scent of fresh cedar filled her nostrils. Julia had always loved cedar, so Mary wasn't surprised she'd chosen it. Then she went to the dresser and opened each drawer. At the Schofield's house, she had a very small stand with a single drawer and a wardrobe about half the size of this one. Her bed was more like a cot rather than the luxurious one in this room.

Lester returned with her trunk that was only half full since she had so little. "That thing isn't nearly as heavy as it looks. If you need anything I will get someone to take you to town."

Mary smiled and nodded. She had very little cash to purchase anything, and she wasn't about to ask Lester for money.

As if he could read her mind, he dug in his pocket and pulled out some money. "You might want to go tomorrow since I wasn't sure what you would want to cook."

"Who will take me?" she asked.

"Julia said she would, if that is all right with you."

Mary couldn't help but smile as she nodded. It was better than all right with her. "That will be great."

"Pick up something nice for yourself while you're there. Julia said that women like pretty things ..." He pursed his lips. "And I wouldn't know what was pretty if it smacked me in the face."

His choice of words made Mary chuckle. "I'm not one who has to have new things, but thank you anyway."

Instead of accepting that, he glared at her. "I said to buy something, and that's exactly what I want you to do."

Mary had never been talked to like that before, and she didn't like it a bit. She glared right back at him. "I may be your wife, Lester, but let's get something straight. You are not to speak to me in that tone of voice. I did absolutely nothing wrong, and I am not a child." As soon as those words left her mouth, she gasped. What was she thinking?

Chapter 3

He blinked a couple of times and then shook his head. "I am very sorry, Mary. You have to understand that I have never had a wife before."

"And I have never had a husband before. But that doesn't—"

"I said I'm sorry." The contrite look on his face let her know he meant it.

She nodded. "Yes, of course. Apology accepted."

"But I really would be happy if you would pick up something—even if it is a small thing—as a gift from me." His expression softened. "A wedding gift."

"I have nothing for you."

"*You* are my wedding gift."

Mary's heart melted. That was probably the sweetest thing anyone had ever said to her.

"Will you do that for me?"

A lump formed in Mary's throat, rendering her unable to speak. So she just nodded.

"Good. Now that we have that settled, I would like for you to cook some supper with whatever you can find in the pantry."

His tone had gone back to being gruff, but it wasn't as intense, and it didn't bother her as much now. Mary understood that he had a lot of things to learn about being married, and she intended to help him figure it out. And maybe while she was at it, she'd learn a thing or two.

*

Lester wanted to kick himself for the way he'd been acting with Mary. He knew better than to speak to her in such a mean-spirited tone.

His apology was sincere, but it was hard for him to back down. He'd never been good at saying he was sorry. However, he knew that if he didn't do it now, she might never warm up to him.

As soon as he walked outside, he stopped, lowered his head, and prayed—something he didn't do often enough. *Lord, I know You are aware of everything. Please don't give up on me. I want to be a good man ... a good husband. I want to love Mary and for her to love me.* He opened his eyes and thought for a few seconds before continuing his prayer. *I pray that You will make me think before I speak and help me to become the man You want me to be.*

After he finished praying, he put the horse and carriage in the barn. He had a few more chores to do before he could go back inside. Hopefully, Mary would be able to find something to do with the sparse offerings in the pantry, but if she couldn't, he decided he would accept that and try his best to be as nice as he possibly could.

An hour and a half later, he decided it was time to call it a day. As he walked toward the house, he started feeling an odd sensation—that maybe Mary would let him know she'd thought things over and that she now realized she made a huge mistake, and she wanted to go back home to Virginia. After all, why would anyone want to be with a man like him? He was grouchy, not particularly handsome, and his house wasn't even finished.

By the time he got to the front porch, he had braced

himself for whatever she might say. He paused for a second and then plowed forward. As soon as he opened the front door, the aroma of something cooking accosted his senses. Mary had clearly managed to put some of the pantry items together for dinner.

He walked quietly through the house, got to the door of the kitchen, and stood there, watching her as she stirred something in the pot. When she turned around, she jumped.

"How long have you been here?" she asked.

"Just a few minutes. What are you cooking?"

"I found some jars of beans and some cornmeal." She gave him an apologetic look. "I hope it's okay that I used the little bit of ham that I found."

"That is fine."

"I need to make a list for when I go to town tomorrow." She turned and stirred the beans in the pot. "Do you have seeds for planting?"

"Isn't it too late?" he asked. He'd given up planting a garden after his last disaster.

She shook her head. "No, there are still some things that can be harvested quickly."

"Maybe you can ask Julia if she has some seeds that she can spare."

Mary nodded. "She probably does. My sister is very efficient."

"When will supper be ready?"

"Not too much longer. I believe the beans are ready. All we have to do is wait for the cornbread to finish baking."

"That is good. I will go to my room and change clothes." He started to walk away but stopped and turned around. "Do you need any help?"

She glanced over her shoulder and gave him another of her odd looks. "No, everything is fine here."

He gave her a clipped nod before leaving. Once he got to his room, he sighed. He didn't have much experience with women, but he still knew that Mary was different. She obviously had thoughts and opinions. And for some strange reason that he didn't understand, he wanted to know what they were.

*

The next morning, Julia showed up at the front door. Mary couldn't remember ever being so happy to see someone. She hugged Julia and pulled her into the house.

"You look so happy," Mary said. "Marriage certainly agrees with you."

Julia smiled and nodded. "Stone is a wonderful man, and he treats me like a queen." She glanced around. "Where is Lester?"

"He went to the gold mines." Mary glanced down at the floor and then slowly raised her gaze to her sister's. "He gave me some money ... a lot of it. I am supposed to buy food and anything else I want."

"That's good." Julia didn't appear the least bit fazed as she put her hand on Mary's shoulder. "Are you having a difficult time accepting the money?"

Mary nodded. "It doesn't seem right."

"I know. I felt the same way when I first came here. Stone gave me everything I needed and most of what I wanted. I felt guilty at first, but after much prayer and seeing how he truly felt, I have accepted the fact that this is one of the things the Lord has blessed me with."

"It doesn't feel right accepting so much when Papa is still struggling back home."

"Sit down for a minute," Julia said. "There is something I want to tell you."

Mary did as she was told. After they were both seated, Mary looked at her sister and waited.

"Papa knows that Stone ... well, he is a man of means. Stone offered him some money, but Papa turned him down."

"Why would he do that?" Mary asked.

Julia shrugged. "Pride, I'm sure. He wrote Stone back and said he didn't want to take money that isn't rightfully his."

Mary shook her head. "That is fine for him, but how about Sarah? She still lives with Papa."

"Is she worried?" Julia's forehead crinkled.

"No, I don't think she has any idea how difficult things have been for Papa. He can tell her all day long that he doesn't have enough money for food, and she will turn right around and ask what he wants her to cook for supper."

Julia's lips twitched. "As I recall, Sarah only knew how to cook a couple of things, so the choices are limited."

"That is still the case. But Papa doesn't seem to mind."

Julia stood. "Why don't we discuss this more later? We have a lot to do in town. Go get your things, and we can be on our way."

A few minutes later, they were on the road leading to town. Julia chattered about all of the exciting things she'd learned about Golden, some of the friends she'd met, and the church she attended.

"Pastor Ledbetter and his wife seem very nice," Mary said.

"They are. Mrs. Ledbetter has been a tremendous help to me. In fact, she reminds me of Mama."

"Yes, I agree. I thought the same thing when she hugged me. In fact, she even smells like Mama."

Julia leaned back and laughed. "I think it's the vanilla flavoring she puts behind her ears. She said that works better than any perfume she has ever tried, and the pastor likes it too."

Once they arrived in town, they went from one shop to another, until they had everything Mary needed and wanted for the house. "I have never been able to spend so much money in one day …" She opened her purse. "And I still have money left over."

"Now we need to find something nice for you," Julia said. "How about a dress for you to wear to church?"

"I don't know—"

Julia gave her a look that silenced her. A new dress

would be good since the outfits she had brought were rather tattered and worn looking.

With Julia's help, she found something pretty in a light shade of blue. "This is a wonderful color on you." Julia turned around. "Now we need to find something for your hair."

"No, I can't—"

Once again, Julia leveled her with a look. "How about that clip over there?" She pointed to a shelf beside the clerk's desk.

By the time they were on their way back to the ranch, Mary had a new outfit, complete with the hairclip and shoes that were prettier than anything she'd ever owned. The only thing stronger than the guilt she felt was the giddy feeling of having new things.

"I think you will be surprised by how pretty you look," Julia said as she pulled up in front of the house. "Let's get these things put away so you can start supper. Stone is feeding the children some soup I started before I left, but I have to be back home to help put the children to bed."

As soon as Julia left, Mary got busy in the kitchen. It took her almost an hour to have everything simmering and baking.

The shadow that fell over the kitchen a couple of hours later made her turn around. Lester folded his arms and widened his stance. "Did you get everything you needed in town?"

Her lips twitched with nervousness as she nodded. "Yes, I bought plenty of food to stock the pantry and a few things for the kitchen."

He lifted an eyebrow. "Did you get yourself something?"

She cast her gaze downward and nodded. "I did."

"Are you ashamed?" He took a step toward her.

"A little bit."

"I don't understand why. I thought women liked to get new things."

She opened her eyes wider and looked directly at him. "I have never had the means to get many new things. Money has always been tight for Papa, and we barely had enough to buy food, let alone personal belongings."

"I understand that, but it is different here. I have enough money to get you whatever you want, and I don't ever want you to feel ashamed."

His voice still sounded gruff, but Mary heard something different now. In spite of his gravelly voice, she heard compassion—a trait that caught her off guard.

"Thank you."

He turned his attention to the stove. "When are we having supper?"

"It should be ready in about an hour. I'm baking a pie for dessert."

An expression of surprise and joy came over him, and her heart melted. "Pie? That makes me very happy." He paused. "In the future, I would like for you to prepare such a big meal earlier in the afternoon for dinner, and we can eat a lighter supper."

She nodded. Although she had never lived on a ranch or farm before, she understood that was the way things were done. Papa liked a larger meal at night because he had to bring his dinner to work.

Lester came back into the kitchen and sat down at the table as she put food on the plates. When he lowered his head to say a private blessing, she cleared her throat. He looked up at her.

"Is something wrong?" he asked.

"I would like for you to say the prayer aloud for both of us."

He blinked and then nodded. "Yes, I will do that."

After the blessing, he didn't waste any time before taking his first bite. She held her breath until after he swallowed and smiled at her.

"Do you like it?" she asked.

His smile broadened. "Yes, this is delicious. You are a very good cook."

It made her happy to see him enjoying his meal. She ate the food on her plate before standing to carry her dish to the sink. He asked for more.

After he finished dessert, he got up and studied her as she washed the dishes. "Did you need anything else?"

"No, I have everything I need … for now." He cleared his throat. "I think I will go to my room. Tomorrow comes awfully early."

Once Mary was alone in the kitchen, she let out a long sigh. Although Colorado was quite different from what she was used to, she could actually envision herself liking it here eventually.

The rest of the week went by in a similar fashion. Each time Lester let Mary know something he liked—whether it was food or how she wore her hair—she made sure to repeat it. After all, he was extremely generous, and although his grouchiness came and went, his good moods lasted a bit longer. And he didn't lose his temper again, although she suspected he was sometimes on the verge of it.

When Sunday morning arrived, Mary stood in front of her wardrobe and stared at her new dress. This was the first time in years she would put on something new, and her apprehension gave her pause.

What if the dress didn't fit as well as she thought it did? What if it wasn't suitable for church? What if Lester hated it?

As tempting as it was to fall back on something she felt comfortable in, she forced herself to put on the new dress. She stood in front of the mirror and stared at herself, wishing one of her sisters could be here to give her the confidence she lacked.

"Mary, are you almost ready?" Lester bellowed. "We need to leave soon."

"I'll be out in a few minutes."

She picked up her comb, arranged her hair as Julia had,

and fastened the clip. Then she powdered her nose and took one more look in the mirror before forcing herself to leave the safety of her room.

As soon as Lester saw her, she knew he noticed something different. Not only did he do a double take, he smiled. "You look lovely, Mary."

Her cheeks flamed. "Thank you." She noticed that he was dressed in something different as well. "So do you."

He chuckled. "No one has ever told me I look lovely before."

"I should have said you look handsome." Those words didn't come easily to Mary, but she suspected it had been difficult for him to tell her she looked lovely.

They rode to church in a comfortable silence. Mary wondered if this was how it was between other married couples. She cast a self-conscious glance in her husband's direction.

He looked over at her. "Is everything okay, Mary?"

She nodded. "Everything is just fine. I'm just a little bit nervous."

"But why? This is church. No one should be nervous at church."

"I know," she said. "But the only church I have been to is the one back home …"

"And?"

She shrugged. "During the time I took care of the Schofields' children, I didn't go every Sunday."

He lifted his chin. "Then perhaps that is why the Lord pulled you away from there and sent you here. He has commanded us to worship Him."

Mary hadn't thought about it like that, but maybe Lester was right. "At least Julia will be there."

"And you know Pastor Ledbetter and his wife."

"Yes. They are such nice people. I look forward to hearing his sermon."

"I hope you like to sing."

125

Singing had always been one of Mary's favorite things to do—both in church and with the children. She'd been told she had a nice voice.

They arrived a few minutes before the services began. Julia stood outside the church waiting for them. As soon as Mary and Lester walked up, Julia pulled them inside and gestured toward the pew. "Have a seat. I need to find Stone and let him know you're here."

Mary was pleasantly surprised by how warm everyone was. People greeted her and welcomed her to Colorado. No one seemed fazed by the fact that she didn't even know Lester before she came. In fact, she learned that several of the women had been mail order brides, and they seemed happy with their husbands.

When church was over, Julia introduced her to more people. The whirlwind of so many new people at once had her head spinning, so she was happy when Lester approached and said they needed to leave.

"You looked as though you needed rescuing," he whispered on their way to the carriage.

"I don't know how I'll remember all of their names."

"Don't worry about it. Everyone will understand if you have to ask them again." He helped her into the carriage and then went around and got in on the other side. "By the way, you have a beautiful singing voice."

"Thank you. That's the one thing the Lord has blessed me with."

"The one thing?" He slowly shook his head. "No, I believe that the Lord has blessed you abundantly with many things."

She gave him a curious look. Most of her life, she'd felt as though the Lord had overlooked her when it came time to hand out His blessings.

"First of all, you are a lovely woman with strong features." He smiled. "I like that in a person. Secondly, you are a wonderful cook."

"Thank you."

"Stop thanking me." His growling voice that had once startled her made her laugh. "What is so funny?"

"Nothing."

"It must be something, or you wouldn't be laughing. Tell me."

She took a deep breath and turned to face him. "Do you really want me to?"

"Yes, I wouldn't have said it if I didn't."

"Okay, here goes. Most of the time you seem angry. At first, I didn't know what to think, and I was a little bit frightened."

"Frightened? Of me?" He sounded surprised.

"You have to remember that I haven't been around many men. Papa is very soft-spoken, and Mr. Schofield was rarely around. The household staff didn't talk much."

Lester guided the horse to a clearing, stopped, and turned around to face her. "Mary, you need to remember that I haven't been around many women either—especially since I came here. The only ones I've seen for the past several years have been at church, and only on Sundays."

She nodded. "Yes, I am aware of that."

"I would never do anything to hurt you, so please don't be afraid of me." He gently lifted her hand and kissed the back of it. "I want to protect you. Even though we haven't known each other very long, I am happy that you are my wife. I have to admit that I was nervous about sending off for someone. I was willing to settle for whatever came my way, and when you got off the train, I couldn't believe my good fortune."

"Your good fortune?" She looked into his eyes and felt an odd sensation in her abdomen. "What are you talking about?"

"One look at you, and I was instantly smitten."

"You were?" She gulped as she looked at him in shock. "With me?"

He nodded. "Yes, with you. I realize that you don't see yourself as pretty, but I think you are attractive, and you have a sweetness that I don't deserve."

All of Lester's kind words went straight to Mary's heart. "This is a lot to take in, Lester."

"I know. But I want you to know that there is no doubt in my mind that I will grow to love you with all of my heart. Now all I can do is pray that you will love me in return."

She smiled up at him but didn't say a word. She prayed for the same thing.

*

They easily fell into a routine during the following week. Early Saturday afternoon, he came inside, found her in the kitchen, and took her by the hand. "I'm taking you to town. We need to pick out some things to make our house look like a home."

The fact that he said *our* rather than *my* when referring to the house warmed her heart. "What kinds of things?"

"How would I know? That's why I waited for you to come so you could pick something that would make you happy." His gruff tone had returned, but now it didn't sound so bad.

Chapter 4

"Do you like that?" she asked, pointing to a picture.

Lester narrowed his eyes and tried to see it as an object of beauty, but he had no idea what he was doing. "If you like it, let's get it."

She smiled and shook her head as she moved on. "Can we get a new serving platter? I would like to have my sister's family over for dinner soon."

"Get whatever you want. That's why we're doing this."

After they finished purchasing what she wanted for the house, she expected him to steer the carriage toward the house. But he didn't. Instead, he pulled up in front of the clothing shop and instructed her to get another dress.

"But I don't need one," she argued.

"Just get one. I'll wait out here."

Without Julia to help her, Mary had no idea what to do. But she didn't want to argue with her husband, so she went inside.

The sales clerk smiled. "I remember you. What can I help you with?"

Fortunately, the clerk had listened to Julia and remembered all they'd discussed, so she was able to help

Mary choose something nice. "I believe you look best in pastels, like powder blue and soft pink. If you stay with those colors, you will do just fine."

With slightly more confidence than she'd had earlier, Mary went back out to the carriage where Lester waited patiently. "That was fast. Are you all set?"

She nodded. "Thank you for being so generous."

After they got home, Mary put her dress in the wardrobe and started decorating the house, while Lester headed out to the barn to feed the animals. Mary had seen him tending to the animals, and she was amazed by the difference between his tenderness with them and his gruffness with people. Maybe one of these days he'd be consistently pleasant with her, although that didn't seem likely.

Even though she'd seen his softer side, she still found herself tensing up when he walked into a room—at least until she could tell what kind of mood he was in. She wished she could talk to someone about it, but she didn't want to sound ungrateful.

Before they went to their own rooms later that night, Lester told her he wanted her to wear her new dress. She nodded her agreement and then went to her room while he stood there watching her.

The next morning was a repeat of the previous Sunday. They arrived at church, talked to a few people, sat with Julia's family, listened to the sermon, sang hymns, and then went home. Only this time, Lester didn't stop to tell her sweet things. Instead, he drove the horses as though he couldn't wait to get back.

She put the food on the table as quickly as possible. He ate without saying much, and then he got up and changed to do some work in the barn. Mary went to her room to rest since she didn't want to do housework on the Lord's Day.

As she lay in her bed, staring up at the ceiling, she thought about how time had passed since she'd been in Colorado. Yet not much had changed, except she wasn't quite as afraid of Lester. She'd originally thought she'd have more time with her sisters, but it didn't work out that way. Both of them had their hands full with family matters, and Lenora lived on the other side of Golden.

That night, Mary prepared some soup and cornbread for their supper. She was concerned that Lester might not consider that adequate, but he ate it quickly and didn't complain.

The next morning he got up, drank a cup of coffee and ate the eggs and biscuits she placed in front of him. After eating, he stood up and announced that he would be in the gold mines for most of the day. She nodded before turning back to her housework.

She finished her housework by mid morning and suddenly found herself with nothing to do. This was one of those times when the loneliness crept over her, and she wished she could be back home in Virginia. She sat down at the kitchen table, folded her hands in front of her, and dropped her head forward to pray. She asked the Lord to show her His hand in her life.

It was another beautiful day, so she wandered outside. She could see the cows grazing in the pasture. The horses spent most of their time in the barn, so she decided to go see about them.

The barn was dreadfully quiet, so she tiptoed over to the closest stall where Lester's favorite horse stood looking as lonely as she was. "Hi, Brownie," she whispered. "Are you hungry?"

The horse turned and looked at her before resuming his original position. It was almost as though he was ignoring her.

She walked past his stall to the next one where another horse, this one named Grady, stood. He wasn't quite as tame as Brownie, but he seemed happier to see her. So she decided to have a chat with him.

As she patted his nose and ran her hands along the side of

his face, she started out telling him how beautiful he was. He seemed to enjoy it, so she continued.

"If I were as pretty as you, I would hold my head high and strut around town, letting everyone know I was there."

He whinnied, and she laughed.

"You know what I'm talking about, don't you?" She turned around and found a stool to sit down beside him. "I guess you probably don't understand what I'm doing here, so I'll tell you. It all started when …" She talked about how she'd lost her job and had to move back in with Papa and Sarah. "I know Papa loves me, but I wish he could have figured out another way." She paused. "It's not that I don't appreciate Lester. I do. It's just that I don't feel like I would have been the girl he would have chosen if there had been other possibilities."

She nuzzled the horse. "I know I'm not beautiful, even though he told me he thinks I'm attractive. And I don't see how he could love me since he barely knows me. After all, the only times we're together are during meals and church. Other than that, he is always working, and I'm always here, doing … Who knows what?"

She sighed. "Maybe I should just consider myself blessed by the fact that I have a roof over my head and food on the table. Girls like me don't deserve anything else."

"Oh, but I disagree."

Mary's head jerked up. The voice came from the door of the barn. It sounded sort of like Lester, but it was softer and gentler—even more than when Lester didn't sound so gruff.

As Mary quickly stood and moved around behind the horse, she cleared her throat. "Who is that?"

The silhouette of a man framed by the bright light of the sun behind him moved closer, and she grabbed the horse's mane. By the time he got to the edge of the stall, her heart hammered so hard she was sure he could hear it.

"It's me, Lester."

"What are you doing here? I thought you said—"

"I decided to come back home and do some work here. I thought you might enjoy going for a ride in the carriage this afternoon."

"Oh." Shame filled Mary as she thought about all the things she'd said, thinking that the horse was the only one who would hear.

*

Lester had gotten close enough to see Mary's wide-eyed face. She appeared frightened, almost as though she were afraid of him.

"I heard what you said, Mary. Are you unhappy here?"

She looked him in the eye and opened her mouth, but nothing came out. Her chin quivered as her eyes misted over.

His heart ached at the sight of the distraught woman he'd married only a few weeks ago. He took a step toward her, until she visibly tensed.

"Mary, I want you to be happy."

He could see that she tried to smile, but now the tears flowed down her cheeks. Without another thought, he closed the distance between them and pulled her into his arms.

"My sweet Mary, you have been through so much." He held her out enough to look at her face. "What can I do to make things easier for you?"

"Nothing." She sniffled. "It's just that—"

"You are lonely, aren't you?"

She hesitated only for a moment before she nodded. "Maybe a little."

He squeezed his eyes shut and said a silent prayer for the Lord's help. When he opened them again, he leaned over and kissed the top of Mary's head. He knew by now that he'd already started falling in love with her, and now all he wanted to do was make her love him back.

"Would you like to visit Lenora?"

Her eyebrows went up just enough to know he had her attention. She looked into his eyes.

"But she's so far away," Mary argued.

"Not that far. It won't take us more than an hour or so to get to her husband's church."

"Do you know where it is?"

He nodded. "I went there once with Stone before he met Julia."

"Are you sure you don't mind?"

Seeing the new hope etched on her face, he wouldn't have minded doing anything that made her happy. "Go do whatever you need to do, and I'll get one of the horses ready."

"Can we take Grady?"

He tilted his head as he glanced over at the horse he hardly ever rode or hooked up to the carriage before turning back to her. "If that is what you want, that is what we'll do."

Mary lifted her skirt and scurried out of the barn. He watched until she disappeared inside. Then he went about the business of getting Grady ready for the ride to the other side of Golden.

He made sure to add an extra blanket in case they didn't make it back home before the sun went down. Even though it was late June, some of the nights could be rather cold.

It had become painfully obvious that he hadn't done a very good job of making Mary feel welcome, and now he intended to change that. Mary hadn't had an easy life in the past. Even though Lester didn't doubt that her father loved her, he didn't understand how the man could have sent his daughter off to marry someone, sight unseen.

When Mary came out wearing her blue dress she'd picked out when she went to town with Julia, he couldn't help but smile. That dress was beautiful on her, and he intended to let her know how he felt.

She gave him a shy smile. "I'm ready."

He looked at her with admiration. "You look lovely, Mary."

"Thank you." She started to get into the carriage, but he stopped her.

"Let me help you up." He gently lifted her and placed her in the seat beside his. Her eyes widened, but she smiled her gratitude. "I am bringing some extra blankets in case it gets cold."

He went to his side and got in. "Let's go see your sister. I can't wait to meet her after all the good things I've heard."

*

Mary stared at her husband. She couldn't think of anything sweeter he could have done but this. And it was all for her.

"I appreciate what you're doing, Lester."

"My pleasure." He smiled. "I want my wife to be happy."

The look in his eyes let her know that he meant those words. She felt a twinge of something inside her chest as she continued looking at him. Lester wasn't the most handsome man she'd ever met the first time she saw him, but he was getting better looking as each day passed. And now he was one of the best looking man she'd ever seen.

"Do I have something on my face?" he asked.

She let out a nervous laugh. "Nothing but kindness."

His grin widened. "That's good. You deserve kindness, sweet Mary."

At that moment, something had changed … something significant … something life changing. Mary knew that she was falling in love with this man who, in spite of his crusty exterior, had a kind heart and the willingness to provide a good life for her.

They made small talk most of the way to Lenora's house. Lester spotted the church and pointed. "That is where your sister's husband preaches."

Mary had goose bumps on her arms at the very thought of seeing the sister she hadn't seen in years. "I hope she is home."

Lester nodded. "Me too."

He pulled up in front of the church and got out. "Wait right here. I will go inside and see if Pastor Grant is here."

She nodded. Almost the instant he disappeared through

the double doors of the church, she noticed movement out of the corner of her eye. She turned and saw a woman coming straight toward her, and based on the way she walked with purpose, Mary knew it was her sister.

Mary jumped out of the carriage and ran straight toward Lenora, whose eyes popped open wide. "Mary!" Lenora opened her arms wide and pulled Mary close. "I have missed you so much."

"I've missed you too."

"What are you doing here?" Lenora glanced around. "Did you come alone?"

"No, Lester is inside the church looking for your husband."

"Good," Lenora said. "I'm sure Jesse is talking his ear off, so we'll have a chance to catch up."

"Where is Andrew?"

"He is inside the house. When I heard someone coming, I told him to wait inside for me."

Mary slowed down and tugged at Lenora's arm. Lenora turned around and gave her a curious look.

"How is everything for you?"

"What do you mean?" Lenora asked.

"Do you like it here? Do you like being married? Is your husband good to you? How is he with Andrew?"

Lenora tipped her head and laughed. "Slow down, Mary. I can only answer one question at a time."

"Sorry." Mary offered an apologetic grin. "I'm just trying to figure out what I'm supposed to be doing."

They got to the bottom of the stairs to the parsonage. Lenora stopped and turned toward Mary.

"Why? Is what you are doing not working?"

Mary closed her eyes and shook her head. "I have no idea. This whole thing is so new to me. I never thought I would ever be married. In fact, I am probably the most improbable bride you have ever met."

Lenora laughed. "You are being silly, but I suppose that

is what makes you so charming."

"Charming?" Mary sighed. "That has never been a word I would have used to describe myself."

"Well, take it from me. You are very charming." Lenora reached out and smoothed Mary's hair. "And you are very pretty."

"Now I know you're delusional. My hair is dull, and my eyes are too far apart."

"No, your hair is not dull. You have obviously never seen how it glistens in the sunlight." Lenora paused. "As for your eyes, they are wider-set than the rest of ours, but that is what gives you a mysterious look."

"Mysterious?" Mary had never heard that before.

"Yes." Lenora took both of Mary's hands in hers and squeezed. "All your life you have focused on others and denied yourself. I am sure that Lester sees your beauty, or he would never have sent for you."

"He didn't know me before I arrived."

"Did you not know that Julia and Stone gave him a photograph?"

"Photograph?" Mary frowned. "I don't remember—"

"It was one of all four of us. Stone said that he chose you because of a combination of your attractiveness and intelligent expression."

"Oh." Mary glanced down. He had told her she was attractive, but she didn't believe him. "Well, I suppose I still have a lot to learn."

"Believe me, we all do."

The sound of a door opening caught their attention. "Mama, is it okay if I play outside for a little while?"

Lenora grinned at Mary before turning to Andrew. "Just for a little while, but first, come say hello to your Aunt Mary."

His eyebrows shot up. "Aunt Mary?" Next thing Mary knew, Andrew had run toward her and practically thrown himself at her.

She laughed. "It is so good to see you, Andrew."

He looked up at her with a curious expression. "You are not as tall as you used to be."

Mary laughed again. "I am the same height, but you have grown. It won't be long before you're looking down at me."

He smiled up at her before running toward the barn. Lenora turned back to face Mary.

"Andrew is enjoying his life here. At first, I wasn't sure if this was such a good idea, but once Jesse and Andrew warmed up to each other, no one would know that Jesse wasn't Andrew's original father. Andrew even calls him Papa." Lenora touched Mary's arm. "So tell me exactly what is bothering you."

It took a while for Mary to explain everything. Lenora nodded at times and asked a few questions. After Mary said all she needed to say, Lenora motioned toward the rocking chairs on the front porch.

They sat down and rocked in silence for a few minutes. Mary remembered that Lenora always did this when she needed to think.

Finally, Lenora glanced up at her. "What you are going through is perfectly normal. You said that you have seen moments of kindness and that his grouchy demeanor isn't as bad as it once was."

Mary nodded. "But I'm afraid of making him angry."

"Are you sure you're afraid of him?" Lenora asked. "Or are you worried that he doesn't think you are perfect?"

"No one is perfect."

Lenora nodded. "That is what I keep trying to tell you. Even though you say those words, I have never known anyone who expects so much from herself as you do."

"So how can I fix that?"

Lenora chuckled. "There you go again—still trying to achieve perfection." She took a deep breath before continuing. "Why don't you tell Lester that you would like to have a talk? Tell him what you just told me and hear what he has to say. I suspect he can dispel your worries better than I can."

"That's it?" Mary tilted her head. "That's all I have to do?"

"I didn't say that was all, but it is a good place to start. When he tells you something, really listen. Let all of your bad thoughts about yourself go. No one else sees you as you do."

"Okay. I'll try to do that."

"I hope you are staying for supper. We generally eat early because Jesse has to get up with the chickens to visit some of the elderly members of the congregation. He tries to see them all at least once a month."

A few minutes later, Lester and Jesse walked up to the house. Jesse greeted Mary with a hug. "It's nice to meet another sister-in-law. Lester here has told me that he is enjoying getting to know you."

Lenora nudged Mary and whispered, "See?"

The rest of the visit was fun. By the time Mary and Lester were on their way home, Mary felt much better about things.

"Are you happier now?" Lester asked once they were on the road back to their place.

Chapter 5

Lester had prayed for an answer about how to make his wife happy, and the only thing that came to him was bringing her to see Lenora. He waited patiently for her answer.

Finally, she looked at him and smiled. "Yes, very much so."

He nodded and took a few deep breaths before speaking again. "I have been concerned that you are unhappy with me."

She quickly turned to face him. "I thought—" She stopped talking and looked down. "I was worried that you regretted sending for me once you saw me."

"Not at all. In fact, I was pleasantly surprised."

"By what?" she asked.

"First of all, the way you look. I could tell that you were attractive from the picture, but in person, you are … well you are downright pretty." He grinned at her, and she blushed. "And when I tasted your cooking, I was even happier."

"Really?"

He nodded. "I wouldn't lie about such a thing."

"What else?"

"You want more?" he asked.

"Only if there is more."

"Oh, trust me, there is." He told her several things he liked about her, including her intelligence, the way she moved with efficiency, and how she didn't expect too much from him. Then he pulled over and turned to face her. "Now it's my turn. Do you have any regrets?"

Her lips quivered, and she gave him an apologetic look. "Well, I sort of did … at first. I thought you were terribly grouchy, but later, after I mentioned it, I saw you get nicer and nicer."

"I'm sorry I was so grouchy."

"I know." She sighed. "And you are handsome too."

He couldn't help but laugh. "Handsome? Me?"

She nodded. "Yes, and somehow you get more handsome everyday."

His heart melted as he met her gaze. "No one has ever told me that before."

"There's another thing I like about you."

"What is that?"

"You are a very generous man. At first, I didn't know what to think or why you were so free with your money. But now I see that it is your nature, although I am still uncomfortable taking it."

He picked up her hand and kissed the back of it. "You are not taking my money. You are my wife. It is *our* money."

A grin slowly spread across her face. "I can tell you really mean that."

"I do. And there is something else I really mean."

Her eyes widened. "What is that?"

"This." He reached for her face and cupped it with both hands. And then he gently pulled her toward him for a kiss. When she responded, he pulled her close and kissed her again. "Would you consider joining me in my room soon?"

She relaxed against his chest and sighed. "Is tonight too

soon?"

Lester's heart soared. "Tonight is perfect."

Mary pulled her head away and looked him in the eyes. "Shouldn't we be getting on home? It will be dark soon."

"Of course."

As they rode the rest of the way home, they chattered about a lot of things. Lester learned quite a bit about his wife, including the fact that she was open to having a family—a very large family—with him. And he couldn't think of a time he'd ever been happier.

Sarah's Suitable Marriage

Hollister Sisters Mail Order Brides

Debby Mayne

He that believeth on the Son hath everlasting life: and he that believeth not the Son shall not see life; but the wrath of God abideth on him.

John 3:36

Chapter 1

(April 1887, Virginia)

Sarah held the curtain back as she watched Papa come up the walk toward the front door. When she didn't see that familiar conspiratorial smile he wore when he brought home news to her sisters that they were about to become mail order brides, she let out a breath of relief.

As soon as he opened the door, his exhausted gaze met hers. "What's for supper?"

"Ham and potatoes."

"When did you learn how to cook ham?"

Sarah glanced down. "I didn't. One of the ladies from the church brought it over."

"I told you not to take handouts. I have my pride, you know."

She forced a smile to try to ease his mood that was obviously pretty sour at the moment. "I picked up some chocolate for later."

He narrowed his eyes. "Chocolate's expensive." The growling tone of his voice made her insides churn.

The backs of Sarah's eyes burned, but she willed herself

not to cry. "I know, but it's not like we have it every night."

Without another word, John Hollister headed back to his room as he did every evening after work. Sarah knew he'd be back out in just a few minutes, expecting his dinner to be on the table and ready to eat.

Papa's moods had grown progressively worse. Gone were the days when he came home with a smile and a story from his day at work.

She hastily scooped food onto plates and set them down. By the time she had the forks and knives in place, he appeared, shaking his head as he did so often lately.

"I don't know how we're going to make it, Sarah. Folks are losing their jobs, and I think I might be in the next round." He grimaced as he adjusted his position in the chair. "I'm getting too old to be doing the job, so I can't expect them to keep me around much longer."

"You're not old, Papa." Sarah tried to keep the lilt in her voice, but she knew she wasn't successful. All her life, she'd been the happy sister and rarely worried about anything. But times were different now. She realized the dire straits they were in, and it was impossible to pretend any longer.

"You might not think so, but I am." He took a bite of his ham, chewed, and swallowed before leveling her with one of his steely gazes. "I don't know what it is about you that has the men looking elsewhere, but unless you find a man soon, I'm afraid we'll have to find you some paid work ... and you know how difficult that can be in this town."

"I love children. Maybe I can do what Mary did."

Papa waved his free hand around. "Then by all means, do it. What is stopping you?"

Sarah sighed. She had tried to get a job watching children as Mary had before she was sent off to marry Lester Packard in Colorado, but when asked about her experience, all she could talk about was the limited amount of time she'd spent with her nephew, Lenora's son, Andrew. And that was never enough since all of the other people competing for the job were much more experienced.

"I'm afraid that if we don't find a way for more money to come into the household, we will wind up ..." Papa shook his head as he gave her the most pitiful look she'd ever seen on his face. He stood up, threw his napkin down on the table, and walked back to his room.

Sarah felt a huge burden swelling in her chest. Papa had tried so hard for so long to make ends meet, but as time went on, his pay kept getting lower, but their expenses continued to rise. She would have done anything to make things better for him, but she had no idea what to do except try again to find a job.

The next day she walked from one business to another, begging for work. But no one was willing to take a chance on hiring her. She'd never felt so hopeless in her life.

*

(Golden Colorado)

Marvin had just gotten back from the general store he owned when his brother Oliver rode up on his horse. Marvin glanced up and grinned, but the serious look on Oliver's face let him know whatever he'd come to talk about was no laughing matter.

"What's wrong with you?" Marvin asked.

"Nothing's wrong with me." Oliver got off the horse and stood there staring at Marvin. "It's you."

"Me?"

"Yes. You've been single long enough. It's time for you to get a wife."

"What brought this on?"

"After we saw you last, Anne and I both noticed that you were becoming set in your ways and hard to communicate with. A wife would help."

Marvin chuckled. "Where do you recommend I look for someone who is willing to be married to me and live all the way out here in the middle of nowhere while I'm either in town at the store or working on the ranch?"

Oliver narrowed his gaze and stared at his brother. "The same place most of us find our wives."

"Uh-uh, not me. I'm not about to send off for a mail order bride."

"That's ridiculous," Oliver said. "There are no single women in town, but there are plenty of them back East who are willing to take a chance and come here."

Marvin shook his head. "Nope." He headed toward his cabin before he stopped and turned to face Oliver. "I'm perfectly fine as I am. Want to come inside for some food?"

"What kind of food?"

Marvin shrugged. "I still have some from the basket you and Anne sent a few days ago."

"That's another thing I'm talking about. The only meals you get are what people send you. What happens if people stop giving you baskets of food?"

"I don't know. I'll deal with that when it happens." He planted a fist on his hip. "Well, are you coming in or not?"

"No," Oliver replied. "I'm going home to a fresh, hot supper prepared by the loving hands of my wife." He smiled. "If you change your mind about sending for a bride, let me know."

"Why? Do you already have someone in mind?"

"Maybe. If you're ever serious, let me know, and I'll tell you." Oliver paused. "By the way, Anne said for me to let you know that you are invited to our house for dinner after church on Sunday."

Marvin tipped his head. "Tell Anne I will be there."

"I'll do that." Oliver got back on his horse, and without another word, he rode away, leaving Marvin standing there staring after him.

When Marvin finally went inside, he took a long look around. The cabin was sterile. There was very little furniture, and his kitchen table looked pathetically bare. He'd eat some of the beans and biscuits his sister-in-law had prepared, and then he'd go to bed. Alone.

Yes, he was lonely. Although he didn't like admitting it, even to himself, he knew it was long past time to find someone to share the rest of his life with. But he didn't like the idea of a mail order bride. What if he didn't like her? What if she found him repulsive? That was a huge chance to take just to have someone to call his wife.

*

After church on Sunday, Marvin rode his horse to his brother's family's house. On the way there, he marveled at the scenery that was still untouched, with the wide-open spaces and the mountains that offered a breathtaking view.

Oliver was outside when Marvin arrived. "The children are happy you'll be here for dinner. William wants to know if you can teach him how to carve with his new knife."

Marvin chuckled. "I thought that was a father's job—to teach his son those things."

"It is, but I thought it would be good for his uncle to spend some time with him."

Marvin narrowed his eyes. He knew Oliver well enough to know when he had something up his sleeve, and he suspected this was one of those times. But he still liked the idea of spending time with his nephew, so he nodded. "I will do that after dinner."

Anne peeked out from the doorway, her face lit up in a big grin. "I'm glad you could make it, Marvin. Dinner will be ready in about an hour."

Marvin smiled back. "I'm looking forward to it. You're one of the best cooks I know."

"That's just because you don't get many healthy meals." Before he had a chance to respond, Anne looked at Oliver. "Would you mind taking the children for a few minutes? Margaret helped me with the pies, but she's getting mighty squirmy."

Oliver laughed. "We'll be happy to." He nudged Marvin.

"Right?"

"Yes, of course."

A few minutes later, Oliver went over to the side yard to play a game of ball toss with William while Marvin swung his niece around in circles. When he stopped, she giggled and begged for more. After about fifteen minutes, Marvin and Oliver switched places. When the children had enough, both of them went up to Oliver and leaned into him.

"Just think, Marvin, you can have your own children someday if you will give in and take a wife."

Marvin studied the picture of family happiness with his brother, niece, and nephew all clustered together. At this moment, the idea of having his own family did appeal to him, but he knew there was more to having a family than enjoying playtime with them.

Anne called them to dinner, so the children raced each other to the door. Oliver took advantage of a little bit of alone time with Marvin. "My favorite day is Sunday. Nothing brings me more pleasure than taking the family to church and then spending the rest of the Lord's Day showing them how loved they are."

Marvin started to say something, but a lump formed in his throat, and he decided against it. The emotion he'd felt when the children screamed with laughter as they played together was strong. Maybe he should consider finding a wife soon … but not now.

Throughout dinner, the children mostly behaved, but occasionally, he noticed that they would grab something when their parents weren't looking. He found that amusing. When they saw that he was aware, their eyes widened, and he winked.

After dinner, he spent a little bit of time with William, teaching him the basics of carving. Margaret watched for a little while but quickly lost interest and went and got her doll. This family setting overwhelmed Marvin more than he thought it would—so much so that he decided to let Oliver know his thoughts.

"I think I might be ready to find a wife soon," he told Oliver before he left. "Just give me a little more time to think about it."

"Let me know when you decide, okay?"

Marvin nodded. "You will be the first to know."

*

The instant Papa walked through the door six weeks later, there was no doubt in Sarah's mind what was about to happen. The look on his face was one she'd only seen three times before, and it was always when he found husbands for her sisters. She swallowed hard, closed her eyes and prayed she'd know what to say, and then forced a smile.

"Beautiful day," Papa said. "As soon as I get changed, I have something to discuss with you." He disappeared into his bedroom.

Sarah's heart grew heavier by the second as she imagined all sorts of things and prayed that she was mistaken. But that wasn't likely. Papa had made it clear that he couldn't afford to continue taking care of her. She'd tried some more to find paid work but to no avail. The writing was on the wall that she would be on her way somewhere she'd never been to marry someone she'd never met. The very thought of that frightened her.

As the youngest of four sisters, Sarah knew she'd been pampered. The others had tried to teach her things that Mama had been unable to after she'd gotten sick, but they quickly lost patience after some brief, futile efforts. And then Mama passed away, leaving the entire family in a numb panic.

Sarah knew she wasn't the best cook in the world, but she'd gotten a little bit better over time. At least now she rarely burned the biscuits. Although Papa ate everything she put in front of him, she suspected it was more from hunger and not wanting to waste food than actually liking what she'd prepared.

Occasionally, someone from the church would bring them something, but that wasn't enough to keep them fed. Papa gave her a tiny amount of money to purchase essentials. She did her best, which wasn't good enough. They almost always ran low on food before he got paid again. In fact, there were a couple of times when she had to go outside to pick some dandelion greens to cook with the onions in the pantry. Mary had taught her how to sauté them with butter to get rid of the bitterness.

She had just put the plates on the table when Papa came out of his room waving an envelope. If she'd had any doubts before, they were now squelched.

Chapter 2

"I have the ticket to your future right here in this envelope," Papa said.

"I will not become a mail order—"

"Before you argue with me, I want you to know that I have very carefully selected the person who will be best for you." He lifted his chin. "I insisted on finding you a good provider who will treat you well."

Sarah tried hard to remain silent, but that was impossible, given how upset she was. "How would you know who is best for me?"

Papa shook his head as he sat down and picked up his fork. "This young man owns a general store, and he has a ranch and cattle. According to his brother, he doesn't expect his wife to be an expert cook, or for that matter, a great housekeeper. All he wants is a Christian woman who is willing to give him children."

Sarah was so upset she couldn't say a word or swallow the first bite of the dinner she'd cooked. She just shoved the food around on her plate with her fork.

"His name is Marvin Olson. His brother Oliver has a nice wife and two children. Oliver claims that Marvin is very good with the children, and he is an excellent businessman."

Sarah blinked as she looked into her father's eyes. That was when she saw a flash of regret. "Do I have to go?"

Papa sighed as his shoulders sagged. "No, you don't have to go. But it might be worth going there to at least meet him."

"What if I go and find that I don't like him?"

"Then we will decide what to do then." Papa cleared his throat. "I did make it clear that the final decision must be yours."

"Where is this man?" Sarah still didn't want to go, but she was curious about where her father was trying to send her.

"Golden Colorado, where your sisters are."

She lifted an eyebrow. "So I would get to see Julia, Lenora, and Mary?"

Papa nodded. "Yes, in fact, he has talked to Julia's husband Stone about having you stay at their house until after the wedding."

"In that case, I'll go."

"That's not all," Papa said as he leaned back and stared at the envelope. "This Marvin Olson has said that if things work out, I may come later and work at his store."

"But you have a job here ... and a house. What will you do about that?"

Papa shook his head. "You already know that I am not sure how much longer I will have a job, and with all of the younger people starting families, I think I will be able to sell this house fairly quickly." He paused.

Sarah knew that Papa never wanted to leave Virginia, so the situation must have been direr than she realized. There was nothing she could do or say to change that, so she finally nodded.

"When will I leave?"

"Next week."

Sarah closed her eyes to think without seeing Papa's sad eyes staring back at her. When she opened them, she saw that he was staring at the wall.

*

Marvin felt Julia's excitement as she stood next to him, waiting for the train to deliver her sister. He still had some reservations, but if this young woman was anything like the sisters he knew, she would be sweet, smart, and interesting. He had made it very clear that although he bought the train ticket for Sarah to come to Colorado, there were no guarantees of a wedding. He wanted to meet her first to make sure they got along.

"You will like Sarah," Julia said for the third time. "That is, as long as you don't expect someone who can do more than the basics around the house. I will teach her how to cook a few more things, and if she needs me to help with the cleaning, I promise I will do that."

"Cooking and cleaning aren't that important to me. I just want someone who will be a good mother."

"Sarah is excellent with children."

"I know," Marvin said with a smile. "You have told me that many times."

"I'm sorry, but I am so excited to have all of my sisters nearby. I miss them so much."

"How long has it been since you last saw Sarah?" he asked.

"Six years," she replied. "Six very *long* years."

The sound of the train tracks rumbling brought them back to why they were at the station. "Then I will let you greet her first," he said. "I'll step over there so you can have some sisterly time before you bring her to me."

She gave him a quick smile and nodded. "I appreciate that."

After the train stopped and the passengers disembarked, Marvin felt his pulse quicken. The very notion that he was about to see the woman who would most likely become his wife sent a myriad of emotions through him—excitement, fear, joy, dread, and curiosity.

He had seen photographs of Sarah, so he knew she was a lovely woman. But when he spotted her standing on the top step looking around, his heart felt as though it would pound right out of his chest.

She was the most strikingly beautiful woman he had ever seen in his life. Her strawberry blond curls framed a fair-skinned face with perfectly shaped lips. Her eyes were wide and framed by long eyelashes. Julia had already told him that Sarah had light brown eyes with flecks of gold, sometimes making them appear greenish. The closer she got the smaller she seemed. And when she walked into her sister's arms, he realized just how petite she was.

After their warm embrace, Julia looked around until she met his gaze. He was grateful not to have had to move from where he stood. Julia took Sarah by the hand and led her to him.

Sarah didn't bother trying to hide her evaluation of him. He watched as she looked him up and down and then met his gaze with a smile.

"It's nice to meet you, Mr. uh ..." She glanced over at Julia who nodded. "Marvin." She extended a gloved hand.

He took her hand and gave a slight bow. "It is nice to meet you too, Sarah. How was your trip?"

She rolled her eyes in a comical way. "Exhausting. I used to think I would enjoy riding a train, but if I never see the inside of one again, I'll be just fine." She turned to her sister. "I'm starving. I hope you have food at your house."

Julia tilted her head back and laughed. "I do have food at the house for supper, but I also have something in the carriage."

Sarah grinned at Marvin. "My sister remembers that I have a voracious appetite."

Marvin did remember Julia talking about Sarah enjoying her food, but to look at her, he would never have known. She was very slim. In fact, the only thing about her that didn't appear perfect was that she was a little bit too thin. However, he also knew that her father was poor and couldn't afford to purchase enough food for the both of them.

"Are you hungry now?"

She gave him a curious smile before she tilted her head back and let out a raucous laugh. "Hungry? Why, I'm always hungry."

"Would you like to eat what your sister brought or perhaps stop in town for something to eat?"

Her eyes widened. "Like at a restaurant?"

"Yes, that's what I was thinking."

"I would love that!" She let out a sigh of contentment. "I have only eaten in a restaurant a couple of times in my life, so it will be fun."

He studied her face and nodded. "Then let's do that before we go to your sister's house." He glanced over at Julia who appeared to be watching with amusement. "Is that all right with you?"

"Absolutely. What time can we expect you to be at the house?"

"We won't be long. After we have dinner in town, I thought I would show her my store and then we can go to your house."

"Why don't I take her things?" Julia asked. "I can put them in the room where she'll be staying."

Marvin loaded Julia's carriage with Sarah's trunk and bag before leading her to his carriage. She paused long enough to let him know she needed help, so he lifted her up before going around to his side.

He'd been warned that Sarah was helpless, but until now he didn't realize how much so. Now he wasn't so sure he'd made the right decision to bring her here.

*

Sarah liked Marvin. Although he wasn't the best looking man she'd ever seen, he was kind and made an effort to help her feel comfortable. In spite of his scrawny frame, she could tell he was much stronger than he looked. And his eyes were a nice shade of blue beneath eyebrows that were much too bushy for his long, narrow face. He had a very sweet smile.

As they rode along, she decided to relax a little. She removed her bonnet and tossed her waist-length strawberry blond hair over her shoulder.

Marvin gave her a sideways glance and then did a double take. He smiled again, causing her pulse to quicken. "You have very pretty hair."

"That's what people tell me, but I don't see it. I think my hair is a mess."

"Then why don't you cut it?" He focused his attention on the horse that he was guiding, but she could sense the amusement in his tone.

"Cut my hair? Seriously?" She shook her head. "I wouldn't want to look like a man."

He chuckled. "Sarah, my dear, you couldn't look like a man if you chopped off all of your hair and put on dungarees."

She giggled. "Now that would be a sight, wouldn't it?"

Marvin nodded but still didn't look directly at her. "It would indeed."

Sarah remembered something she and Papa had discussed. "My father said that you might have a job for him in your store."

Again, he nodded. "Yes, that is very likely ... that is, if things work out between you and me."

She tilted her head and stared at him. "Why wouldn't it?"

He pursed his lips, forced a smile, and glanced at her. "I don't know. We'll just have to see."

"But I thought—" She sighed. "Oh, never mind." Papa had told her she didn't have to go through with a wedding, but she didn't believe him.

One thing she knew for sure was that Papa had started planning his move out west. He said that all it would take to begin his journey was one more pay cut because he couldn't afford to feed just himself on any less than he currently earned.

Maybe Marvin didn't like her. She liked him well enough so far—much better than she expected. As they continued to ride along in silence, she thought about all the things she could do to make him like her more.

"What is your favorite food?" she asked.

His forehead crinkled as he glanced at her again. "My favorite food?"

She nodded. "Yes. If you were told you could have one thing to eat, what would it be?"

"Can this be a meal, or does it have to be just one food?"

Sarah pondered his question before responding. "It can be a meal." She'd have to spend some time with Julia in the kitchen and really pay attention this time.

"I suppose it would be ham, sweet potatoes, and cornbread."

"Then that is what I will cook for you after I get settled." Sarah smoothed her hands over her dress and glanced away. The terrain was very unlike anything she'd ever seen before. The ground seemed much harder, the land more vast, and the mountains much taller than the hills she was used to.

"What else can you cook?" He smiled and looked at her with a knowing expression.

She was tempted to tell him she could cook anything he wanted, but she'd never lied before, and she didn't want to start now. "Look, Marvin, I'm not very domestic. In fact, I never stuck around in the kitchen long enough to get a proper cooking lesson. But I'm a grown woman now … about to be married … At least I think I am." She looked at him, hoping for a positive sign. But she didn't get one.

"Do go on," he urged.

"It's high time I learn to cook a decent meal."

"And how do you plan to do this?"

"Julia will teach me."

He slowly nodded. "I see."

"Why are you acting like you don't think I'll do it?"

His chest expanded as he took another breath. Sarah didn't know why his opinion meant so much to her, but it did. "I never said I didn't think you would do it. All I said was—" He cut himself off. "Let's not do this right now. We barely know each other, and it doesn't seem that we're getting off on the right foot."

"Okay." Her voice came out barely above a whisper. The feeling she had right now was similar to how she used to feel when she did something Papa didn't approve of.

When they arrived in town, she looked around at everything and everyone. It was quite different from Virginia where people dressed in their finest suits and dresses to go to town. Here they didn't seem too concerned with appearances. Sarah wasn't sure how she felt about that.

He pulled up in front of a hotel that had a sign in the window indicating that there were no vacancies and another sign that read *Café*. "I hope you're hungry," he said. "They have some mighty fine food here."

He got out and started toward the building before stopping, turning, and coming back to the carriage to help her out. Together they walked inside.

The entrance took Sarah's breath away with a blend of elegance and rugged western style. One look around let her know this place would be expensive.

"We don't have to eat here," she said softly.

"I thought you wanted to." He looked at her with a curious expression.

"It looks expensive."

"It is, but it is not something I do all that often. It's okay to spurge once in a while."

When they sat down, she picked up a menu and stared at it before lifting her gaze to his. "One meal costs more than a whole week's worth of groceries," she said. "I can't—"

"Nonsense. You are hungry, so I want you to eat."

She licked her lips and looked back at the menu. There

wasn't a single thing on the menu that seemed reasonably priced. "What can I have?"

"Anything you want."

"Why don't you order for me?" she finally said as she shoved the menu toward Marvin.

"I don't know what you like."

"I am not picky. I'll eat anything."

Chapter 3

After a meal of veal and potatoes with onions, Marvin helped her back into the carriage. He couldn't help but smile at the look on her face when she first tasted her food. She stopped eating for only a second to announce that it was delicious, and then she devoured it in half the time it took him to eat his meal. Where she put all that food, he had no idea. She'd clearly been ravenous after that long train ride.

"Do you go there often?" she asked once they were back in the carriage.

"No, but when I do, I always enjoy it."

She leaned back and closed her eyes. "I don't think I have ever tasted anything so good." She swallowed hard. "Or expensive."

Marvin was tired of talking about the money he'd just spent, so he decided to change the subject. "Are you ready to see my store now?"

"Yes, of course."

He turned the corner and pulled up in front of a large building with a sign above the front door. "Here we are, at my general store."

Her eyebrows shot up. "This store is yours?" She looked

at the building and blinked. "The whole thing?"

"Yes. I started out over there." He pointed to a small building across the street. "But business was brisk, and I outgrew that space, so I had this place built to accommodate everything I needed to sell."

"Can we go inside?" she asked.

"Yes, of course. That was what I'd planned to do."

She hesitated only for a moment after he opened the door for her before stepping inside. An audible gasp escaped her lips as she looked around.

"There is so much in here. Where does it all come from?"

Marvin couldn't help but laugh at her childlike innocence and wonder. "Various places. Vendors come here and show their wares. I purchase what I think my customers will like."

"This store has everything a girl could possibly want."

"Well," he said with a chuckle, "I don't carry much food, and I leave the women's apparel to the shop down the street."

"But you have material for making clothes. I don't know why anyone would ever want to go anywhere else to shop."

"Why don't you walk around and see if there is anything you might like?"

"Oh, but I can't afford—"

He interrupted her. "Pick one thing and don't worry about the cost."

Sarah's face turned pale momentarily, but the color quickly returned. She nodded and darted toward the first aisle.

One of his employees, Henry approached Marvin. "Is that pretty young lady the woman you sent off for?"

Marvin nodded. "She is indeed."

"You will have some beautiful children."

"Maybe so …" Marvin took a step back. "That is, if I decide to go through with the marriage."

"If you change your mind, I am sure there will be a long line of young men vying for her attention."

"No doubt." Marvin's initial attraction to Sarah had been

short-lived after he realized how helpless she was, but he didn't need to tell Henry that. "She is a lovely woman."

"I don't know why you wouldn't want to marry her." Henry looked at him but quickly cast his glance away. "I'm sorry. That is none of my business."

"That's quite all right. Just remember that there are many things more important than the way a person looks."

They both turned toward the aisles and watched Sarah as she walked up and down each row, lifting items off the shelf and then putting them back. It took her a while, but she finally approached holding a pincushion.

"I'll take this." She held it up for Marvin to see.

"A pincushion? Why don't you choose something nicer, like a music box or vanity set?"

Her shoulders sagged. "I would, but I think it is more important to be practical, now that I am here to become your wife."

The fact that she had that thought tugged at his heart. "I will buy you the pincushion, but go pick something else … something pretty and less practical."

She scrunched her pretty eyebrows together as she gazed directly into his eyes. "Are you certain that is okay? You won't think any less of me for doing that?"

"Positive. Now go find yourself something nice."

It only took her a couple of minutes to bring back a very ornate mirror. "I like the music box very much, but it doesn't serve any practical purpose." She handed him the mirror. "I have always wanted one of these."

"Now you will have one." He took it to the cash register where Henry rang up the items. After he paid, they walked out of the store together.

"I thought you owned everything in there," she said as he helped her into the carriage.

"I do."

"Then why did you pay for my presents?"

He laughed. "When I take something from the store, I

always pay like any customer would. That keeps the bookkeeping easy and honest."

"I don't suppose I will ever understand." She looked longingly at the bag.

He handed it to her, and she accepted it, pulling it to her chest. "I'm glad you found something that makes you happy."

"This is very nice, but I can't honestly say that it makes me happy."

Marvin gave her a curious look. "But I thought—"

"Oh, don't get me wrong. I like what you bought me—at least I like the mirror." She cast her gaze downward before looking back up at him. "But I know that things can't bring happiness. They just make life a little easier and fun."

He guided the horse toward Julia and Stone's house. "Then what makes you happy, Sarah?"

"Being with my family ... seeing my sisters and knowing that everything will be okay."

Marvin's opinion moved up a bit after that revelation. He suspected that she left out the fact that knowing she'd have another meal also brought her some joy. His heart melted a little for this woman, but he knew better than to let that sway him to do something he might later regret. At least he hadn't made a firm promise to marry her before meeting her.

Julia greeted them as soon as they approached the house. For the first time since he'd met Sarah, she didn't need help getting out of the carriage. In fact, she hopped out so fast he wasn't sure what happened, until he glanced up and saw her running full speed toward Julia.

*

Sarah was so happy to see her sister again she felt as though she might pop. Even though she'd seen Julia at the train station, it was different now. She wasn't starving half to death, and she wasn't in front of a bunch of people she didn't know.

"I have a surprise for you," Julia said.

"A surprise?" Sarah's pulse quickened. She'd already had enough surprises for the day, but another one sounded exciting.

Before Julia got another word out, some people came out of the house, catching Sarah's attention. When she focused her gaze on the porch, she recognized Lenora and Mary … and there was a boy behind Lenora.

"Andrew! I—" Sarah's voice stuck in her throat. Next thing she knew, Andrew had bounded off the porch and was on his way toward her.

She opened her arms wide and pulled him in. "I would give you a swing around, but I'm afraid you're too big for that."

Andrew laughed. "Maybe I should swing you instead."

"You probably could." Sarah turned around to face Marvin who remained standing by the carriage watching. "Did you know my sisters and nephew would all be here?"

She caught the twinkle in his eye as he exchanged a glance with Julia. "Maybe."

Sarah turned around and ran back toward Marvin, throwing her arms around him. "Thank you so much for bringing me here. You have made me the happiest woman in the whole entire world."

She quickly realized he wasn't hugging her back, so she let go of him. He took a slight step to the side.

"I'm so sorry. I couldn't help myself."

"No need to apologize. I can tell you're beside yourself with happiness."

"You asked me earlier if my new mirror made me happy." She waved her arms toward her sisters. "This is what makes me truly happy, all the way down to the tips of my toes."

Julia gestured toward the house. "Let's not stand out here all day. Let's go inside so Sarah can meet my husband and children."

Sarah was delighted to see the children. She knelt down

and talked to each of them, one by one, giving them hugs and laughing as they answered her questions. She glanced over her shoulder every few minutes and saw Marvin looking down at her, watching with an intensity she hadn't seen before. She wasn't sure whether or not she was being judged, but it sure did seem like she was.

"Is anyone hungry?" Julia asked.

Sarah's ears perked up. "I am."

"How can you be hungry after that big dinner you had?" Marvin asked.

Lenora belted out big, hearty laugh. "When you get to know Sarah, you'll realize she's always hungry."

"I know," Mary added. "I can't remember a time when she wasn't ready to eat."

"Stop it." Sarah tried to have a stern face, but she couldn't … not with so many people she loved, all in the same room. "I just have a healthy appetite."

Julia nodded. "I suppose you can call it that. Mary and Lenora, why don't the two of you stay here and get to know Marvin? I would like for Julia to help me in the kitchen."

As soon as they agreed to do that, Sarah followed Julia. "Your house is so big!"

"Yes, I know. In fact, I wasn't sure what to think when I first came here." Julia turned around and placed her hands on Sarah's shoulders. "Well? What do you think about Marvin?"

Chapter 4

Marvin found Sarah's sisters to be delightful women. Julia and Stone were regular customers at the store, and he helped Stone with a few things around the ranch. He'd met Mary before at the church, and he'd seen Lenora from a distance, but this was the first time he'd had the opportunity to actually chat with all of them.

What amazed him the most was Sarah's natural way with the children. She didn't hesitate to get down to their level and meet their gazes. They seemed comfortable with her from the moment they met her. He suspected it had a lot to do with the fact that she was so childlike herself.

As soon as Stone came inside, he fell into a comfortable discussion about the state of affairs in Colorado. They both agreed that there was still money to be made, and the town of Golden would continue to grow. That was good for both of them as businessmen.

It wasn't much longer before Julia came out of the kitchen and called them to supper. When he walked over to the dining room, he saw Sarah putting bowls of food on the table. She glanced up at him and grinned.

"Julia showed me how to cook the peas, and this time I

paid close attention. She said she'll show me how to fix ham and sweet potatoes next time you come over."

Marvin gave her a clipped nod. "That would be nice."

He couldn't help but notice a look of disappointment on her face. It wasn't easy pretending to feel something that he didn't—at least not yet. Every now and then, he felt a little twinge of amusement at her ease with the children and some of the silly things she said, but he knew it wasn't how he was supposed to feel about a woman he wanted to marry.

Dinner was delicious. After he finished, he pushed back from his plate and laid his napkin on the table. "I enjoyed that very much. I'm afraid it is getting late, and I need to go home soon."

Julia smiled before turning toward Sarah. "Why don't you walk him to his carriage?"

Sarah nodded. "Let me carry a couple of plates to the sink first."

"Nonsense," Mary said. "Lenora and I will help Julia clean up."

With a shrug, Sarah turned toward the door and walked outside with Marvin. "I don't think that has ever happened before."

"What's that?" Marvin asked.

"My offer to help clean up was turned down. My sisters used to nag me all the time to do more chores, and now that I'm offering, they're not accepting."

"I am sure they appreciate your offer."

Sarah didn't say anything for a minute, but then she turned around and faced him directly. "Do you like me?"

Her question startled him. "What do you mean?"

"Just answer my question. Do you like me?"

"Yes, I like you."

"But?"

He narrowed his gaze. "Why do I feel as though I did—or said—something wrong?"

"I'm thinking I'm the one who did something wrong, and

I want to know what it is." Her voice quivered.

He looked directly into her eyes and saw the worry that apparently ran deep. "You didn't do anything wrong, Sarah. If anyone did anything wrong it was me."

"That makes no sense. You have been a perfect gentleman by picking me up, taking me to a restaurant and buying me an incredibly expensive meal, giving me gifts from your store, and bringing me here." She sniffled. "If you don't want to marry me now that I'm here, I'll understand."

As beautiful as she was, Marvin had a revelation. He now realized that being young and acting rather childish at times wasn't what bothered him most about her. It was her lack of confidence, and he suspected that her sisters didn't help when they kept shooing her away when it came time for important things.

"Sarah, I think we should get to know each other better before either of us makes that decision." He picked up her hand and squeezed it. "I do like you, but I don't want to jump into a marriage if either of us isn't sure. I suspect you aren't any more sure than I am."

Her chin quivered and then she sighed. "I suppose you are right. It's just that ..." She wiped a single tear with the back of her free hand. "I don't want to disappoint anyone."

"Sarah, my dear, you need to think about your future and what the Lord wants for you." He suspected she had plenty of experience feeling like a disappointment. "We both need to pray about this and then pay close attention to His word. Your sisters will understand either way."

"But Papa—"

"Your father will understand too." He offered her what he hoped was a comforting smile. "Julia has already said that you can stay with her and Stone as long as you like. There is no reason to go back to Virginia unless that is what you want."

*

After Marvin left, Sarah remained in the front yard. She

didn't want to go back inside and face her sisters who would want to know what was going on. She'd never been able to lie, and the very thought of telling them that Marvin wasn't sure she was right for him brought her back to how inadequate she'd felt all her life.

"Sarah?" The sound of Mary's voice caused her to turn around. "Are you okay?"

Sarah nodded. "I'm fine."

"Then what's wrong?"

Sarah cleared her throat. "Nothing is wrong. I'm just thinking about how different everything is here in Colorado."

"Yes, it is, isn't it?" Mary smiled. "What do you think about Marvin?"

"He seems like a nice man." Sarah glanced at her sister but couldn't hold her penetrating gaze that always made her feel like she was being evaluated.

"He would be a good provider."

"I know." Sarah wasn't sure what else to say, and she didn't want to be interrogated, so she decided to change the subject. "What is your house like?"

"It isn't as big as this one, but it is very nice. Lester has let me decorate it how I want, and I am very comfortable there."

"But are you happy?" Sarah asked.

Mary nodded. "Yes, very much so. I wasn't so sure in the beginning, though. When I first arrived, I felt as though I'd made a big mistake coming here."

"Do you ever feel that way now?"

"No, not at all. In fact, I wouldn't want to be anywhere else. Colorado is my home for the rest of my life."

"Looks like it will be mine too." Sarah made a face that used to make her sisters laugh, but it didn't work this time. "Papa might even move here."

"Yes, I know. Julia told me."

"If I don't marry Marvin, I'm not sure he will give Papa a job at his store, so I don't know what he will do."

Mary lifted an eyebrow. "Are you thinking that you might not marry Marvin?"

Sarah shrugged. She hadn't wanted to have this conversation, but since she'd been the one to bring it up, she knew she needed to answer her sister's question. "Neither of us is sure it is the right thing to do."

She stopped talking and studied Mary for a reaction. What she saw surprised her.

Mary actually smiled. "Continue praying for clarity and know that the rest of us will too. We all love you, and we want what is best for you."

A flood of relief washed over Sarah. "Thank you."

"You've lived all your life in our shadows, I'm afraid." Mary gave her an apologetic look. "Now it's time for you to be your own person. Julia and I were talking about how we treated you, and I'm afraid we might have made things more difficult by treating you like a baby."

"Well, I am the youngest of the sisters."

"That still doesn't give us an excuse." Mary put her arm around Sarah. "Just remember that we all have special gifts, including you."

"I've heard that all my life, but I don't know that I do."

Mary chuckled. "Trust me, you do. In fact, I think you and I both have some of the same gifts."

"I would never compare myself to you, Mary. If I did, I would always come up on the low side."

"That is simply not true. You have a beautiful, kind heart, and you're wonderful with children."

Sarah thought for a moment. "I love children."

"And you have a great sense of humor. You have always been the first to laugh and the last to cry."

"That's only because my sisters made my life so easy."

Mary shook her head. "Life has never truly been easy for you … or the rest of us. It wasn't until I came here that I was able to relax and enjoy some of the finer things. The rest of us married good men, and they are able to provide well for us."

"I want what you have, but I'm afraid I might have made some mistakes when I first met Marvin."

"No, Sarah, you didn't make any mistakes. You were just being yourself. That is what the Lord would want you to do."

"Thank you, Mary."

"Do you feel better now?"

"Much better." Sarah started walking toward the house. "I still can't believe what a nice, big place this is ... and I'll have my own room."

"This is a very large house," Mary agreed. "My house is also big, so if you ever want a change of scenery, you may come and stay with me."

They walked into the house when Lenora and her family were about to leave. "We still have a long way to go, so we need to get going before it gets dark."

Later that night, Sarah lay in her bed thinking about the day. As soon as she'd stepped off the train, her life changed. Even if she and Marvin decided not to marry, she knew she'd never be able to go back to where she came from, nor did she want to. Being with her sisters brought her more peace than she'd felt since Julia left.

*

A week later, Marvin trudged into his store. He hadn't seen Sarah since he'd left her sister's house, but she'd been on his mind night and day.

He hadn't been at the store more than a few minutes when one of the other merchants came walking in, his face pinched and his stride hurried. "There's been an accident. Your—" He glanced down and then slowly lifted his gaze to Marvin's.

"What?" He knew it must be serious for the man to look so worried.

"Your brother and his wife were killed in an accident this morning. Oliver died instantly, but Anne survived long enough to get to the hospital. The doc tried to save her, but he couldn't."

"Where are the children?"

"Someone from the church is with them now, but Anne's last words were that you are to take them and raise them as your own."

The rest of the morning seemed to go by in a blur as Marvin closed the shop until Henry arrived later in the day. He went to the hospital where he learned some of the details about the accident. His brother and sister-in-law had been working on something in the barn when one of the beams collapsed and landed on them. Fortunately, the children were inside the house at the time.

Now he had to figure out what to do. He loved his niece and nephew, but he wasn't in a position to be their only parent.

Chapter 5

A couple of days later when Sarah heard the news about Marvin's brother, she had Julia drive her to his house so she could be with him during this difficult time. He might not be her future husband, but she knew he needed comfort and someone to help out with the children.

Marvin kept shaking his head, saying, "It is so unfair. Why did it have to happen to them? Why couldn't it have happened to me instead?"

Sarah rubbed his back as he continued on his rant. When he stopped to take a breath, she spoke. "It is not up to us to decide what is fair but to take over when the Lord calls us to do so. I will help out with the children."

His lips tightened as he looked at her and nodded. "Thank you for that, Sarah. You are a sweet woman."

"And I don't want you to feel obligated to me. I love children, so it will be my pleasure to be there for them while you work and do whatever else you need to do."

The look Marvin gave her was confusing. He held her gaze for a while before a hint of a slight smile crossed his lips. "I will take you up on your kind offer. One of the church members has had them since the accident, but it is time for me to get them."

"When will they be here?"

"I need to go pick them up soon. Would you like to go with me?"

Sarah slowly nodded. "I will be happy to."

Julia glanced back and forth between Marvin and Sarah before speaking. "I will fix supper and either bring it here, or you can come to our house."

"We will go to your house," Marvin said. "I think it will be nice for my niece and nephew to be around other children."

After Julia left, Marvin and Sarah got in his carriage. He didn't talk much, but Sarah understood that he was still in shock over losing his brother. That added to the fact that he was now responsible for two children was quite a bit to deal with.

Margaret and William were huddled together on the floor in the corner of the house when they arrived. The woman who had taken them in explained that they had heard their mother screaming when the barn collapsed.

"Fortunately, someone else from the church just happened to be driving by." She shook her head. "Otherwise, I don't know what would have happened to these precious little children."

Sarah went straight to Margaret and William, put her arms around them, and said a prayer. Then she carefully lifted William and placed him in Marvin's arms before picking up Margaret. "Thank you so much for taking them in," she said.

"I couldn't get them to eat." The woman wrung her hands. "They aren't talking either."

"That is understandable." Sarah hugged Margaret close. "They have been through a lot. It will take time."

Marvin steered the horse, while Sarah clung to the little ones. Not a word was spoken all the way to his house. When they arrived, they brought the children inside.

"I need to get their clothes," Marvin said. "Would you like to stay here with them?"

"Yes, I think that would be best."

After Marvin left, Sarah positioned the children on either side of her and took their tiny hands in hers. She bowed her head and prayed for the Lord to have mercy on them and to help her know what they needed. Then she picked up the Bible she saw on the table. She thumbed through until she found some of her favorite verses since childhood.

As she read them aloud, the children remained very still and quiet. After she finished, she got up and knelt on the floor in front of them. "Would you like something to eat or drink?"

Margaret continued staring at the floor, but William finally spoke up. "When can I see my mama?"

"I'm sorry, sweetheart, but that isn't possible now."

"Who will take care of us?" he asked, his voice cracking.

"Your uncle will take care of you, and I'm going to help." Sarah forced a smile. "Your mother and father loved you very much, and they wanted you to come live here."

Margaret's chin quivered as a tear slid down her cheek. "I want my mama."

Sarah had once felt the same way, and she knew there was nothing she could say to change anything. So she wrapped her arms around the little girl and rocked back and forth. Her heart ached for them. She knew what it felt like to lose a mother, although she'd been older than these children when it happened to her.

When Marvin got back with a trunk filled with the children's clothes and toys, Sarah got up to help put the things away. Marvin sat down with his niece and nephew, but none of them said a word.

Sarah's heart ached for all three of them. She knew it would take some time to return to any semblance of normalcy, and she decided she would do whatever it took to help.

"William, why don't you let your uncle help you find places for your toys, while I go to Margaret's room with her?" Sarah kept her voice soft and light to keep from upsetting the children any more than they already were.

After everything was in place in the spare bedrooms, they all piled into the carriage to go to Julia's house. Stone greeted them at edge of the property. Marvin got out, and the men spoke for a few minutes while Sarah remained in the carriage with the children.

Once they got to the house, Julia took William and Margaret by the hand and led them into the kitchen where her own children waited. Sarah went over to the stove to help her sister put the finishing touches on supper.

Fortunately, the table was quite large, so they were all able to eat together. Sarah was relieved that both William and Margaret ate a little bit.

When it was time for them to go back to Marvin's house, Sarah helped put the little ones in the carriage. "Can you handle everything from here?"

"Yes, I believe so." Marvin took the reins in his hands but continued gazing at her. "Thank you so much for your kindness, Sarah. I don't know what I would have done without you this afternoon."

"I loved helping out."

"Can you come to the house in the morning?"

"Yes." Sarah knew her way to his house by now, and she was certain that Julia wouldn't mind letting her take one of the carriages.

"Would you like for me to pick you up?"

"That would be too difficult for you. I will come there."

Marvin frowned. "I'm not so sure it's a good idea for you to go alone."

"I will be just fine," Sarah tried to assure him, although she did have some doubts in the back of her mind. She took a deep breath, squared her shoulders, and lifted her chin. "You need to have more confidence in me."

A hint of a smile formed on his lips as he gave her a clipped nod. "I will see you first thing in the morning."

When Sarah went back inside, she told Julia her plans. "Yes, of course, you may take one of the carriages. Or I can drive you there."

"No, I prefer to do this on my own."

Julia gave her a look of understanding. "I think that is actually a good idea. You are a grown woman, so there is no reason you shouldn't."

*

When Sarah arrived at Marvin's house the next morning, everything was in a state of disarray. The little girl was crying, and the kitchen was a mess.

He glanced over at her. "I tried to make them some breakfast, but I burned the oatmeal, and now I can't seem to console Margaret."

Sarah did know how to make oatmeal. "Let me take over. Why don't you go on into town and tend to your store?"

"Henry is minding the store this morning. I'll stick around here and do some chores outside if you don't need me to help with the children."

"We'll be fine, won't we?"

William looked up at her and nodded. "I can help."

Sarah placed her hand on his shoulder and gave him a hug. "And I am sure you will be a very big helper."

Marvin cleared his throat. "If you need me, I will be out by the barn."

William broke away from Sarah and ran to his uncle. "No! Don't go to the barn."

Marvin shot Sarah a helpless look. She walked over to William, knelt down to his level, and cupped his chin. "I know you are scared for Uncle Marvin, but he will be very careful." She glanced up at him. "Right?"

Marvin nodded. "Very careful."

Sarah looked at William again. "What happened to your mama and papa is very unusual and probably won't happen again." She stood up. "In fact, I think I will go out to the barn to make sure it is safe. Why don't you stay right here and wait for me until I get back?" She looked at Marvin, hoping he would back her up.

He did. "That is a very good idea. We can wait for Sarah to check the beams and make sure they are strong enough to hold up the walls and roof of the barn."

That seemed to appease William, although he still looked a little uncertain. "Please be careful, Aunt Sarah."

She blinked at the title William had given her. Now wasn't the time to correct him, but she made a mental note to do so later. "I will be."

After she walked outside, she glanced over her shoulder in time to see Marvin step outside with his niece and nephew. With them watching, she walked up to the barn, touched the exterior walls, looked up and down, and then went inside. Although she was doing this more for the children, she could tell that this barn was extremely well constructed. It was doubtful anything would happen to it based on how sturdy the structure looked.

She walked back to the house, smiling. "It is in very good shape ... nice and sturdy."

"Are you sure it won't fall?" William asked.

Sarah hated to make a statement she wasn't completely certain about, but now seemed like a time when she should. She nodded. "Positive."

William's shoulders visibly relaxed. "Okay, Uncle Marvin. But please be extra careful."

Marvin gave Sarah a look of appreciation before he headed out. She saw something else in his eyes, but she couldn't quite put her finger on what it was.

*

The moment Sarah had come back and announced that the barn was safe was when Marvin knew there might be hope for them in the future. He'd witnessed a few touching moments with her relating to the children, but now there was no doubt he could love her if he allowed himself to open his heart.

She might not be the best cook in the world—at least according to her—but that was something she could learn over time. What he appreciated about Sarah was her innate kindness, ability to relate to children, and the way she jumped in to help without any hesitation. Based on Marvin's experience, he knew that children could see right through falseness in adults, and they clearly loved her.

What was even better was that they trusted her implicitly. When she said something, they took her for her word. Now all he had to do was let her know what he was beginning to feel. He hoped she felt the same way about him ... or at least saw potential in a marriage relationship with him.

He did the bare minimum work he needed to do in the barn before he went out to mend one of the fence boards that had come loose. After that, he returned to the house where Sarah had dinner waiting.

"What is this?" he asked.

"Ham and sweet potatoes." Sarah gave him a shy smile. "You said that was what you liked. I am sure I will get better at this, but Julia told me an easy way to prepare it. She hasn't had time to teach me how to make cornbread yet, but she promised she would soon."

Now Marvin's heart completely melted. Not only had Sarah come through for the children, she had actually listened to him and prepared something he said he liked.

The four of them sat down to eat. Sarah cut the children's ham into small, bite-sized pieces and slathered butter over their sweet potatoes. As he started eating his dinner, he thought it wasn't bad.

"Well?" she asked before lifting her own fork. "How is it?"

He smiled. "It is very good. Thank you."

After they ate, Marvin left for the store. "I will be home before supper."

"Take your time." She had started clearing the table. "I will try to get them to have a rest, and then we'll play some games and read the Bible while we wait for you."

Marvin felt an overwhelming sense of relief, knowing that Sarah was watching the children. All afternoon while he waited on customers and jotted down some things he needed to order, he thought about how nice it was to be able to concentrate on the business without worrying.

He was fairly certain now that he wanted to marry Sarah. She had most of the qualities he found important in a wife, and it was a bonus that she was so pretty. He could help her gain confidence over time.

All the way home, he thought about what to say to Sarah and when to say it. And then he prayed for guidance and the strength to deal with whatever she said.

Chapter 6

After they played a couple of games outdoors, they went inside, and she read some scripture that she thought they would understand. Before she was finished, both of them had fallen asleep in the main room.

She stroked Margaret's sweet little face. It broke Sarah's heart that this precious child had lost her mother so young, and she vowed to do whatever Marvin would allow her to do to help her through her childhood. He might not want to marry her, but maybe he would let her be their governess.

She got up and went to the kitchen to start supper so it would be ready when Marvin returned. Every now and then she checked on them to make sure they weren't frightened about being left alone.

The sound of someone approaching caught her attention, and she held her breath until she saw that it was Marvin. Her heart hammered at the sight of this kind man who hadn't flinched about taking on the responsibility of his niece and nephew. Sarah suspected that she could easily fall in love with Marvin if she allowed herself to.

He walked inside the house and chuckled softly at the sight of the sleeping children. "They must have been tired."

"I suspect so after what they've been through lately." She motioned toward the kitchen. "I will have supper on the table soon." She turned toward the kitchen to finish cooking.

"Sarah?"

She spun around. "Yes, Marvin?"

"Can we talk?"

"Yes, of course." The look in his eyes was difficult for her to read. She said a silent prayer that he wasn't about to tell her not to come back.

"Let's sit down at the kitchen table."

"Okay." Now she dreaded hearing whatever he had to say. Papa had always wanted her to sit down when he had unpleasant news for her.

Once they were seated across from each other, he looked directly into her eyes. "Sarah ..."

She blinked but didn't say anything. If he wanted to tell her to leave and stay away, she wasn't going to make it easy. That wouldn't be good for the children. This was a time when they needed some stability in their lives ... and the gentleness of a woman's touch.

"I've been thinking ..." He visibly swallowed hard, closed his eyes as though praying, and then looked back at her.

His hesitation made her nervous. She couldn't very well sit back and wait for him to tell her he wanted her out of his life. "Before you say anything, I just want you to know that I really want to be here for the children. I've been through losing a parent, so I understand what they are going through. It would be wrong for me to—" She crinkled her forehead and paused. "I'm sorry, but I can't help it. What were you thinking?"

An odd expression covered his face. "Please continue. I'd like to hear what you have to say before I tell you what I'm thinking."

"Well, for one thing ..." She tapped an index finger with the other hand. "The children have had such a big loss that I need to be here to help them work through their emotions." She touched the next finger. "And there's the matter of your having to go to the store. Someone needs to be here for them." She gave him a meek smile.

"Is there more?"

She slowly nodded. "There's a whole lot more."

"Then tell me some more."

"Okay, there's also the fact that even if you and I don't get married, I still need to learn how to cook, and I would like to cook for you so you can tell me what I need to do to make it better." She gave him an apologetic look. "That is, if you're willing to do that."

He smiled and nodded. "I am."

"Good. There are other reasons, but I'm afraid I have already dominated this conversation. What, exactly, did you want to talk about?"

A quick smile flashed across his lips, and then he drummed the table with his fingertips. The way he took his time had her holding her breath. Finally, he looked her directly in the eyes. "I would to get married ... that is if and when you are ready."

"You what?" She didn't think she heard correctly.

He shifted in his seat. "I've been thinking about everything that has happened, and I believe that the Lord has made it very clear what He wants us to do."

"Is this something *you* want?" she asked. "Or are you just saying this because you think the Lord wants it?" As she said those words, she realized just how much she wanted to marry this man.

Marvin chewed on his bottom lip for a few seconds before sighing and locking gazes with her. "Both."

"Are you sure you want to marry me?" She couldn't help the fact that her voice squeaked.

He gave her a clipped nod. "I couldn't be more sure of anything. Now I would like to know how you feel."

She blew out a sigh, lifting the tendril of hair that had

fallen in front of her face. He smiled at her, and she smiled back. "I want to marry you too."

His eyebrows lifted slightly. "Are you certain?"

"Yes." She folded her hands in front of her. "You are a very sweet man, and I think you will make a good husband."

"I think you are very sweet too, Sarah, and I would like to be a good husband to you."

"What are we supposed to do now?"

Marvin stood, walked around the table, and awkwardly lifted her to her feet. "I think we're supposed to kiss."

Sarah had never been kissed before, so she let him take the lead. After it ended, her knees wobbled, but he held her up. "Can you do that again?" she whispered.

He laughed and kissed her again. Only this time, she was more prepared. She lifted her arms and wrapped them around him.

"Uncle Marvin, what are you doing?"

Marvin broke the kiss and turned to William who stood at the kitchen door rubbing his sleepy eyes. "I am kissing your Aunt Sarah."

"Oh." Without another word, William turned around and walked back to the front room.

Sarah laughed. "Should we go tell William and Margaret that we're getting married?"

"I don't see why not."

"Oh, before we go in there, when would you like to get married?"

"As soon as we can." He smiled. "Then we can be a family."

*

The next couple of weeks went by quickly. Sarah sent Papa a letter letting him know that she and Marvin had decided to marry. She didn't expect to hear back from him, but she thought he would be relieved at the news.

Marvin had started acting strange about a week ago, but Sarah thought it was probably due to all of the changes in his life. She was feeling rather anxious too. Each day she went to the house that would soon be her home, where she cared for the children, cooked meals, and did housework. And then after supper, she went back to Julia's house.

One bright morning, she went outside to hitch up her favorite horse to one of Julia and Stone's spare carriages. It was a beautiful, clear day that made her appreciate being in Colorado. All the way to Marvin's house, she sang hymns— something she had started doing to entertain herself during the trip. As soon as she got to the edge of the property, she spotted a man standing outside with the children—a man who wasn't Marvin.

Panic rose in her throat. She sped up until she could see who the man was.

"Papa?" She hopped out of the carriage and ran straight toward him, throwing herself into his arms. "What are you doing here? I had no idea you were coming. Did you get my letter?

"Slow down, Sarah." He laughed. "Marvin wanted to surprise you. Looks like his plan worked."

"It most certainly did." She let go of him and took a step back. "How did you manage to come here?"

He shrugged. "My hours were cut again, and I couldn't afford to stay in Virginia. So I asked Julia and Lenora if they knew of anything I could do here. I heard back from Marvin who has offered me a job at his store." He reached for her hand. "He has told me that you are getting married soon, and he would like for me to live on the property to help out around here as well."

"You'll be living in the house with us?" Sarah was delighted beyond words.

"I will be staying here until you get married. And then I'll move in with Julia and Stone and stay there until we finish building a cabin over there." He pointed toward a clearing on the edge of the property.

"Oh, Papa, I can't think of anything that would make my

life any better than it is now." She reached out and hugged him once again.

*

With Papa, Sarah's sisters, their families, William, and Margaret behind them, Sarah and Marvin said their vows in the front of the church. Pastor Ledbetter smiled as he told Marvin to love her as Christ loved the church.

Julia and Stone had Sarah's belongings in their carriage, waiting to take them to Marvin's house. Before they left the churchyard, Julia leaned over and whispered, "We're taking William and Margaret home with us for a few days so you and Marvin can have some time alone."

"You don't have to do that." Sarah sighed. "I have my own family now, and I need to take care of them."

Lenora walked up from behind. "That is all the more reason you need to let Julia take them. You are going to have your hands full for the rest of your life. Take some time to get to know your husband first."

Sarah smiled at both of them and then at Mary who had joined them. Finally, she nodded. "All right. I suppose you know what I need better than I do."

Everyone went to Marvin and Sarah's house to help get her settled. Papa was the last to leave.

"I just wanted to tell you how much I love you and how proud I am," he whispered.

"Thank you, Papa. I'll see you soon." She gave him another hug, and he left.

She turned around to face her new husband whose eyes glimmered with adoration. He extended both hands toward her. "Come here, my love."

As Sarah walked toward Marvin, an overwhelming feeling of comfort and love washed over her. A tear trickled down her cheek.

He cupped her chin and tilted her face toward his. "Why are you crying?"

"Because I am so happy now."

Marvin chuckled. "I've always heard that women can be confusing, so I shouldn't be surprised. Well, my sweet Sarah, I have a surprise for you."

She tilted her head. "A surprise?"

He nodded. "Yes, a surprise for the woman I love." He reached over and picked something up off the table. "I know how much you want to be practical, but you love pretty things. This is my wedding gift to you."

She looked down at the beautiful silver music box she'd seen at the store. "You didn't have to give me this. I really don't need—"

He gently placed his fingertips over her lips. "I know you don't need it, but it is very pretty, and I want you to have it because I love you."

Emotions swelled so big in her chest, she couldn't control herself any longer. She put down the music box, threw her arms around his neck, and squeezed. "I love you too, Marvin. I am so happy I think I might pop."

John's Christmas Bride

Hollister Sisters
Mail Order Brides

Debby Mayne

How on the day that you stood before the Lord your God at Horeb, the Lord said to me, "Gather the people to me, that I may let them hear my words, so that they may learn to fear me all the days that they live on the earth, and that they may teach their children so."

Deuteronomy 4:10

Chapter 1

(Golden, Colorado, August 1889)

John Hollister loved Colorado. From the moment he arrived, he felt as though he'd come home. He looked back over the two years he'd been there and wondered why it had taken him so long to leave Virginia.

He walked out onto the porch of the cabin that Julia's husband had built for him and sat in the rocking chair. This was beautiful countryside that never ceased to take his breath away. The crisp mornings at the foot of the majestic mountains gave him a sense that there was something much bigger than himself to think about.

To top it off, John loved being closer to his daughters. Guilt had plagued him after he'd sent them off as mail order brides, but he didn't feel that he had a choice. Money wasn't stretching as far as it once had, and he couldn't afford to take care of his girls. But now, he lived close enough to see any of them when he wanted, and the bonus was that he had grandchildren who openly adored him.

Sarah's husband Marvin had given him a job running the general store, something he knew nothing about, two years ago. But Marvin was patient, and John caught on quickly. Now the store's profit was doing even better than when he'd arrived, something his son-in-law gave him credit for. John had never enjoyed any job as much as he did this one. He got to see people all day, and his salary was never cut.

The only thing missing in John Hollister's life was a companion. He'd been widowed for quite a few years, but he remembered what it was like to have someone to come home to every day. And he deeply longed for that again.

*

(Georgia)

Nothing in Viola Campbell's life had turned out as she'd expected. Malaria had taken her older brother when she was barely a teenager, her father had died in a train accident, and her mother became very sick, and after several years, she passed away from pneumonia. Now, here Viola was in the family home, alone and lonely.

She once thought she'd marry, but the only man she'd ever loved had met and married someone else. By the time she turned 40, she realized it was probably too late for her. That was such a shame, too, because she had always been so good with children.

"Have you ever thought about becoming a mail order bride?" her best friend Myra asked after church let out.

"That's for younger girls," Viola had countered. "No one would want an old maid like me."

"You never know." Myra shook her head. "There just might be a man who doesn't want a young girl." She gently placed her hand on Viola's arm and looked her in the eyes. "Why don't you give it a try? There's no harm in that, is there?"

"No, I suppose not."

Several of Viola's friends' daughters, including Myra's daughter Grace, had sent their pictures to go into catalogs that went to churches out West. So she'd decided to go ahead and give it a try.

The photo she'd submitted wasn't bad. In fact, it was actually flattering, showing off her strong jawline and thick dark hair that she kept swept up on top of her head. But it still showed her age, something she thought needed to be seen. And even though it was obvious she was older, she added her age to her description to make sure she didn't disappoint anyone who might be interested in a younger woman.

As the weeks passed, she eventually realized that nothing would ever come of her catalog entry. She'd asked that whoever was interested would send a letter in care of her church. After her submission, she'd gone to church early on Sunday mornings, in eager anticipation that someone had responded. But now that several months had gone by with no interest, she'd given up.

On the second Sunday of October, Viola got ready for church as she did every week. As soon as she finished combing her hair and clipping it up, she went into the kitchen and got the pie for the potluck before stepping out into the air that had only recently cooled a bit in the mornings. The past summer had been brutally warm, so she was happy to know that the seasons were changing.

She lived a couple of blocks from the church, so she got there in less than ten minutes. Once she arrived, she brought the pie to the dessert table on the back lawn of the church, where several of the other ladies had gathered.

Myra grinned and waved. She started to say something, but her little grandson came running up.

"Granny, look what I made." He held up a daisy chain with mostly bent or broken flowers. But that didn't seem to matter. He was as proud as he could be.

"Very nice, Robert." Myra scooped up her little grandson and gave him a hug before letting go.

"Where's your daughter?" Viola asked.

"She's having a difficult time," Myra whispered. "Ever since Robert was born, her moods have been rough."

"I have seen that childbirth can cause new mothers to feel out of sorts."

Myra nodded. "I went through it for a few years myself. By the way, have you seen the pastor yet?"

"No, I just got here." Viola turned around and leaned against the table. "Why?"

"He wants to talk to you." Myra gestured toward the door on the side of the church. "Go on in and see what he wants."

"I'm sure it can wait."

"No, go now. He sounded pretty urgent when he came out here looking for you." Myra's lips twitched.

"Do you know what he wants?"

Myra shrugged. "Maybe, but I'm not at liberty to say anything. Go on in and let him tell you."

Viola sighed. Pastor Jennings probably wanted her to head up the next potluck since she didn't have any other responsibilities lately. That was fine, though. She needed something to do to keep her mind occupied.

The pastor's office door on the side of the church building was slightly ajar, so she knocked lightly. "Who is it?"

"Viola Campbell."

"Come on in." His voice bellowed, making her hesitate. "Close the door behind you. I have some news to tell you— something I think you'll like."

"News?" Viola tilted her head. "On a Sunday morning?"

He laughed. "I actually received this on Friday." He picked up an envelope and handed it to her. She glanced down and saw that it had been opened before accepting it.

"Is this for me?"

"It came to my attention, but it is for you." He nodded toward the envelope in her hand. "Go on. See what it is."

She stuck her fingers in the envelope and pulled out a letter. He watched as she read the message. When she glanced back up at him, his grin spread even wider across his face.

"Someone actually wants to marry me?" She swallowed hard. "Someone in Colorado?"

"It appears so," he replied. He opened the top drawer of his desk and pulled out what appeared to be a train ticket, slapped it against his hand, and gave her a more serious look. "This is what you wanted, isn't it?"

"Y-yes, of course. When do I leave?"

"Next Friday."

"But the house—"

"You don't have to worry about the house."

"I don't want to abandon the family home."

He gave her a comforting smile. "We already have someone lined up to purchase your house … that is, if you want to sell it." He paused. "Or if you would like to rent it to the new couple, you may do that and sell it once you are certain you want to stay in Colorado."

She pulled her lips between her teeth and slowly nodded. "That is probably the best thing to do."

"You don't have to worry about a thing, then. My wife and I will take care of everything here. If you decide to stay in Colorado and go through with the wedding, then I will send you the money from the sale of your house."

"And if not?" she asked.

Pastor Jennings shrugged. "We will help the family find another home."

She held his gaze for a few seconds before finally nodding. "That sounds fair to me."

"Okay, then I need to finish preparing for the service. We can talk more after church."

The remainder of the morning went by in a blur. After the service ended, several of the members swarmed Viola, congratulating her and offering assistance. She was clearly one of the last people to learn the news.

*

John stood by the train tracks, fidgeting with the package in his hand. He'd insisted on coming alone to greet his future bride, but now he regretted his decision. What would he say to her? What if he didn't care for her? Or worse, what if she didn't like him?

All of those questions played out in his head until he felt the vibration and heard the sound of the train approaching. For a split second, he found himself hoping she wasn't onboard.

Several passengers stepped down before he spotted her. She looked just like the photo he'd seen, only more attractive. His heart raced until their gazes locked, and then his pulse seemed to stop.

He smiled as he took a step toward her to help her off the step. As he reached for her hand, she tipped her head toward him. "I take it you are John Hollister?"

"Yes, and you must be Viola Campbell."

"Yes, that is correct." She stepped down onto the platform and took a long look around. "So this is Colorado."

"Yes, I am sure you will find it quite pleasant here." As he spoke those words, he thought about how unnatural they sounded. But that made sense because nothing about this situation seemed the least bit natural. "Do you have a lot of bags?"

She shook her head. "Just a couple. I have never found it necessary to have many belongings."

It took them a few minutes get her bags into the carriage he'd purchased with his first paycheck. Then they were on their way to Julia and Stone's house, and John explained the arrangements.

"You will be staying with my daughter in her home."

She narrowed her eyes. "But I thought that was where you lived."

"I have my own cabin on the edge of their property."

"Oh." The look of relief on her face was very telling.

He suddenly became self-conscious. "If this works out for both of us, we will both live in my cabin."

"I would think so." Her cheeks turned pink as she met his gaze. "Tell me about the cabin."

Thankful for something to talk about that didn't require too much thought, he described where he lived. "It is rather large for one person, with two bedrooms, a living room, and a kitchen."

"Do you use the kitchen?"

He grinned. "If you are asking if I know how to cook, the answer is yes."

"A man who can cook." She chuckled. "Imagine that."

"I didn't say I was a good cook. I can make a few things, but most of the time, Julia has me come to her house for meals, or she brings me baskets of food."

"Your letter mentioned that you had four daughters and some grandchildren nearby. Where do they all live?"

John answered her question about how all four of his daughters had moved to Golden, Colorado, as mail order brides. "There didn't seem to be any opportunities for marriage in Virginia."

"Were you concerned about sending them off?"

"Yes, of course, I was. But I prayed about it."

"That is always a good thing to do."

He nodded. "We are all blessed that it turned out as well as it did. They are happy with their husbands and families, which was why I decided that I needed to do something … for myself." He told her more about his daughters—from their personalities to their families.

"They sound wonderful. It must be nice to be able to enjoy your daughters as adults."

"It is." He cleared his throat. "I am surprised that you have never married."

"The opportunity for that passed many years ago."

John sensed that she wasn't telling him everything. He decided not to press for more since he wasn't sure of the details. If she wanted to tell him whatever it was, she could in her own time.

Silence fell between them for a couple of minutes before he decided to tell her more about his own life. "I was married to a very sweet woman who became sick. After she passed away, I went through life in a blur." He gave her a brief glance before turning his attention back to the road. "I don't know what I would have done if it weren't for my daughters."

"I hope they are not disappointed when they meet me. I am probably nothing like their mother."

"They won't be disappointed. I have been alone so long, I am sure they are more concerned about my happiness than having another mother."

"That's good."

"We're almost there." He pointed to the right. "As soon as we get around that hill, we will be on the property. I'll take you straight to Julia's house and help you get your things put away."

She nodded and patted her bag. "I brought something for the children."

Chapter 2

Viola had to stifle a gasp as they approached the large, rambling ranch home. This was the biggest house she had ever seen.

"Here we are." He gestured toward the house where a woman and a couple of children stood waiting on the front porch. "Your home until we are married."

Before she had a chance to say a word, the woman stepped off the porch and walked toward them. "Papa, what took you so long to get here?"

John hugged his daughter and the children who clustered around him. The smallest one, a girl, gave her a dubious look before reaching for him to pick her up. Viola was amazed by how easily he lifted the child.

The woman turned around, grinned, and extended her hand. "I'm Julia."

Viola had to take a breath to calm her nerves as she took Julia's hand. "I'm Viola."

Julia glanced at her father and then at Viola. "Is that what you would like for us to call you?"

"Yes, of course."

"Then follow me, Viola. I'll take you to your room."

Viola glanced over her shoulder. "My things."

"Papa and Stone can get them for you. You have traveled a long way. You shouldn't have to do anything for a while, so I want you to rest and get used to the new surroundings."

Julia was much more pleasant than Viola had expected, but she was still uncomfortable staying in the home of a complete stranger. Regret welled in her chest as she followed Julia to the very back of the house.

"This is your room," Julia said as she made a grand sweeping gesture. "You should have everything you need, but if not, let me know, and I will see to it that you get whatever you want."

"Thank you." Viola remembered what she had brought. "I have some peppermints for the children. I hope you don't mind."

Julia smiled. "You didn't have to bring them anything, but it is very sweet. Perhaps you can give it to them after supper."

"Okay." Viola took a long look around before turning back to face Julia.

"I'll leave you alone so you can get settled." Julia started to walk away but stopped momentarily "Supper will be served in about two hours."

"Do you need any help in the kitchen?"

"No, I already have everything cooking. Just come on out and follow the noise."

After Julia left and closed the door behind her, Viola spun around and took everything in. This room was much nicer than her room back home. John never told her his family was wealthy.

Viola walked over to the wardrobe and opened it. The scent of cedar wafted toward her nostrils. She had always thought she wanted cedar furniture, but it wasn't anything she thought she'd ever be able to afford.

Then she remembered that this wasn't where she would live if she stayed in Colorado. John had already described his cabin. Although it sounded nice enough, based on his description, she didn't think it would be anywhere near as nice as this house.

She opened her bags and hung all of her dresses. Then she put the rest of her belongings in the drawers of the dresser. In the corner stood a small vanity—another piece of furniture she'd always dreamed of having but never dreamed it would be even a temporary reality.

After everything was put away, she lay down on the bed to shut her eyes for a few minutes. The train trip was long, and she hadn't been able to sleep very well with the noise and excitement.

Viola awoke to the sound of someone pounding on the door. She sat up in bed and blinked a few times before she remembered where she was.

"Supper is ready." The demanding voice on the other side of the door didn't sound a thing like Julia.

"I'll be there in a minute." She stood up and walked over to the vanity where she took a quick glance at herself.

"We can't wait all night."

"Can you give me about five minutes?" she asked as she pulled the clip from her hair, picked up her brush, and started working on the tangles.

"That's fine. Just don't take forever."

The last thing Julia needed to do was upset anyone in John's family. So she did her hair as quickly as possible, smoothed her dress, and headed toward the noise.

One glance around the room startled her. All of the strangers stood there staring at her. She didn't see John at first, but when he stepped forward, she let out a quick sigh of relief.

"Okay, everyone, you can quit gawking now." John held up his hands. "This is Viola Campbell. Give her some time to get to know you." He turned to one of the young women who had a toddler clinging to her leg. "Sarah, why don't you talk to her first since you seem to have so many questions?"

"Yes, of course." As soon as Sarah spoke up, Viola recognized the voice from the other side of the door when she'd been sleeping. "Come on, Viola. Let's go in the parlor so we can talk."

"No," Julia said. "Not until after supper." She leveled Sarah with a stern look. "You can wait and give her a chance to breathe before you start your inquisition."

Sarah's shoulders dropped. A man holding a baby approached from the side. "Sorry about my wife. She has always been very direct, and she hasn't been feeling well lately." He held the child up so Viola could see her. "This is our little girl Abigail. She is five months old."

Viola grinned at the child. "Hello, Abigail. You sure are a cute little girl."

Abigail turned away from her father and buried her face in his shirt. He gave her an apologetic half-smile. "She's shy."

Even though Viola had never had children, she'd been around enough of them to know that he was right. "Then I won't try to force myself on her."

Throughout supper, Viola felt that she was on display at the oversized dining table, even though everyone clearly made an effort to keep questions to a minimum. The older children ate with the adults, but the younger ones sat at a child-sized table in the kitchen. Sarah held Abigail as she tried to eat. All of the other sisters took turns going to check on their little ones.

After they finished eating, Julia nodded toward Viola. "You mentioned that you had something for the children."

"Yes." Viola excused herself, went to her room for the bag of peppermints, and came back. As she handed them out, the children smiled up at her. At least she was getting a good feeling from them.

Once all of the children had their candy, Julia stood. "Sarah, why don't you take Viola into the parlor while Lenora, Mary, and I clean up? We'll take care of Abigail."

Sarah hesitated before handing the baby to her husband. "Come on," she said, "I don't like to be away from my baby very long, so let's get this over with."

They'd barely sat down when Sarah tilted her head forward and glared at her. "Why did you come here?"

Viola blinked. "I thought you knew."

Sarah waved her hand. "I know you came to marry Papa, but what are you running from?"

"I am not running from anything."

"Why would you come all the way here just to get married?"

Viola hadn't expected this, but she knew that she needed to defend herself. "For the same reason you did."

"I didn't exactly have a choice." She narrowed her eyes even more. "Someone made you come?"

"No." Viola remembered John telling her that his daughters weren't happy about leaving Virginia. "What I should have said was that I wanted to find someone to spend my life with … a companion. There was no one suitable back home."

"But why did you choose my father?"

Viola could already tell that this was a no-win situation, so she just smiled and stood. "I didn't choose him. He chose me. And if you don't mind, I would like to help your sisters finish cleaning up."

"Why would you do that?" Sarah asked. "Julia didn't ask you to."

"Because I like to help out wherever I can." Before Sarah had a chance to say another word, Viola left the parlor.

*

John noticed the strained look on Viola's face as she approached. He knew that she'd been in the parlor talking to Sarah, so he decided to ask his youngest daughter if she knew what was happening.

She was still sitting there, arms folded, staring at the wall when he walked in. From the look on her face, he knew something was wrong.

"What do you think of Viola?" he asked as he sat down in the chair adjacent to hers.

She shrugged. "She's okay, I guess."

"Do you not like her?" He needed to know if there was a problem before it was too late.

"Why don't you ask her?" Sarah got up. "I need to see about Abigail. She's been teething."

After she left the room, John let out a deep sigh. Sarah used to be so happy-go-lucky and slightly spoiled, but ever since Abigail had been born, she'd been moody and somewhat short-tempered. When he asked Marvin if he'd noticed, he was met with a long look and silence. John suspected his daughter's husband had no idea what to do, so he didn't say anything.

Finally, he got up and went back out to join the rest of his family. At least Lenora and Mary were able to hold a conversation with Viola. And they seemed to like her.

After most of the family left, he asked Viola to join him out on the porch. "Well, what do you think so far?"

She looked out over the vast horizon for what seemed like an eternity before slowly turning around to face him. "I am not sure it was such a good idea for me to come here."

He felt as though something had kicked him in the chest. "Why? What happened? Don't you like it here?"

She closed her eyes and slowly shook her head. "It's not that I don't like it here. It's more a matter of whether or not your family is ready for you to have another woman in your life."

"I have been alone for a very long time."

"I know you have, but your daughter … well, it isn't easy for anyone."

"Which daughter are you talking about?" He was certain it had to be Sarah, but he wanted to know for sure.

"It doesn't matter, John. All of your daughters are lovely women, but they are at different places in their lives. They have such fond memories of their mother that I don't know if anyone will ever be good enough for you … at least not in their eyes."

"Their mother was a beautiful, kind woman, but she isn't here anymore. I think they would want me to be happy."

Sarah gave him a subtle smile. "The question is can you be happy if your daughters are upset with you?"

He swallowed as he thought about her question. Finally, he just glanced down at the porch floor. "I don't know."

"It would be a good idea to know before we move forward with a wedding, don't you think?"

John slowly nodded as their gazes locked. "I suppose you're right. I don't want to upset my daughters."

Her slow smile warmed his heart. She clearly saw some things he had tried to ignore before he sent for her. When he told his girls about Viola coming, Julia and Lenora seemed fine with it. However, Mary and Sarah tried to talk him out of it. Mary eventually acquiesced and said she understood, but Sarah continued to balk.

Chapter 3

Viola's heart ached for this man who clearly loved his daughters but still wanted a life for himself. By the same token, she understood Sarah who was afraid she'd lose her father to a strange woman.

But there was nothing she could say to ease his mind, so she decided not to try. Now all she could do was pray for the Lord to guide all of them to do His will.

"You look tired," she said softly.

He nodded. "I am."

"Why don't you go on back to your cabin? We can't make any decisions tonight, and you could use some rest."

"How about you?" he asked. "You came all this way to a place you've never been before. I don't want you to have to deal with—"

"I'll be fine."

"Are you sure?"

She nodded. She didn't want to make his anguish any worse than it was. The look on his face broke her heart. John Hollister was clearly an honorable man who loved his family—something that came as a relief but reminded her that there was a force here much larger than her.

"As I said, I will be fine," she finally said. "I have overcome more adversity than what I am facing now, and somehow, the Lord has seen me through it."

A hint of a smile tweaked his lips. "Thank you, Viola. You're a good woman. I have to go to work in the morning, but I will see you in the evening."

After he left for his cabin, Viola remained on the porch. She had quite a bit of thinking to do, now that she saw the situation for what it was.

"Is everything all right?"

The sound of the voice behind Viola compelled her to turn around. "Oh, hi, Julia. Everything is just fine."

"What did Sarah say to you in the parlor?"

Viola didn't want to say anything that might cause a rift between the sisters, so she just shrugged. "I'm not sure it's something we need to discuss."

Julia took a couple of steps closer. "Look, Viola, I know that Sarah wasn't happy about Papa taking a wife, but it isn't up to her. Papa has been lonely for quite a while."

"I know," Viola said. "But he doesn't want to upset any of you. He obviously loves his family with all his heart, and he isn't about to do anything to cause more pain than what you've already been through."

"Are you thinking about going back to Georgia?"

Viola turned around to face Julia head on. "I haven't thought that far ahead yet."

"I'm sorry." Julia gave her a look of contrition. "You just got here, and here I am pushing you for answers."

"No need to apologize. You have been extremely hospitable and understanding. I couldn't ask for anything more."

"Maybe Sarah will come around." Julia glanced down before gesturing around the land. "She didn't like this place when she first got here, and now I don't think wild horses could ever drag her away."

"It's different for her, though." Viola paused. "And I am

sure that having her family here made Colorado more attractive to her. Perhaps my coming here makes her wonder if the family relationships will change."

"You are very wise."

"I have seen a lot," Viola said. "A lot of people in my church back home have come to me with various problems—many of them related to family squabbles. Since I'm not the one right in the middle of them, it's easier for me to see what's going on."

One of the children called out for Julia. "I best be getting back inside." She took a couple of steps toward the door before stopping. "I am always up with the chickens, so we can talk more in the morning."

Viola nodded. "That sounds like a good idea. I would like to help you with the housework while I am here. Please don't hesitate to tell me what to do."

"I'll give you some time to recover from the trip first—"

"Don't worry about that. I would actually welcome some work to stay busy."

Julia held her gaze and then nodded. "I understand. Perhaps you can help me with the children."

After Julia went inside, Viola squeezed her eyes shut and said a prayer. She praised God for His holiness and then asked for some guidance for both her and John. *Lord, I want to do Your will.*

*

John headed off to work the next morning with a heavy heart, but by the time he arrived at the general store, he'd decided that all the fretting in the world wouldn't solve anything. He needed to talk to Sarah, and until then, he didn't think it was a good idea to come up with a plan.

The store was busy all day, so time passed quickly. As always, he had a strong sense of accomplishment when he flipped the "closed" sign on the door. Between Marvin's praise and the fact that he stayed busy all day made him as happy as he could be, until he went to his empty cabin each night.

John loved everything about working there—from ordering new merchandise to assisting customers. He was always exhausted at the end of the day, but that was only because he put so much energy into his job.

He'd given very little thought to his personal life during the day, but on his way home, that was all he thought about. There was no telling what Viola thought about a man who allowed his daughter to rule his life.

But he couldn't ignore Sarah's feelings. It was partly his fault that she felt so entitled to inject her opinion into his life.

She'd been the last of his daughters to marry, and until she'd moved out to Colorado, he had let her stay in the family home without too many expectations. Sure, she'd done a little bit of the cleaning and cooking, but she was never very good at any of it.

After she married Marvin, he expected some tension between her and her new husband. Fortunately, Marvin didn't seem to mind the fact that his wife wasn't the best cook or housekeeper. He'd hired someone to come in occasionally to help out.

As he thought about his predicament with his daughter, he reflected on how Sarah had acted ever since baby Abigail had been born. During her pregnancy, she seemed deliriously happy, but the instant her first child made an appearance, something snapped.

Sarah's anger surprised everyone. Unlike before the baby's birth, she was never happy with anything anyone did, but John was thankful that she never took it out on Abigail. In fact, she was the most doting mother he'd ever seen—so much so that it appeared she might smother the poor child.

Mary had come to him with concern about the dark circles she'd noticed beneath Sarah's eyes. "I don't think she's getting much rest," she told him. "And Sarah has always been one to need quite a bit of sleep."

Then it hit him. Sarah had always been grumpy when she

didn't get enough rest. Maybe that was the problem.

Instead of going straight to his cabin, he went over to Julia and Stone's house. His heart skipped a beat when he spotted Viola sitting on the front porch with three of his grandchildren all listening to whatever she was saying.

She glanced up and smiled when she saw him coming. "Come join us," she said. "I'm telling them about life on the farm when I was growing up in Georgia."

"I need to talk to Julia first," he said. "I won't be long."

She gave him a quick nod before turning her attention back to the children. The fact that she was so good with the little ones made him like her even more.

He found Julia in the kitchen, humming while she stirred something in a pot. She glanced over her shoulder when she realized he was there.

"You look mighty happy," he said.

"I am. This is the first time I've been able to cook supper without the little ones tugging at my skirt. Viola has been a tremendous help today."

"That's nice to hear." He cleared his throat. "I've been thinking about Sarah."

Julia made one more circle with the spoon before placing it on the spoon rest and turning around to face him. "I have too. Papa, I really think you need to do what is right—"

He held up his hand to stop her. "You know good and well that I would never do something to upset any of my daughters, now that we are all together again."

"Okay, so what have you been thinking?" She wiped her hands on her apron and gestured toward the kitchen table. "Have a seat?"

Once they were seated, he continued. "Remember how cranky Sarah gets when she doesn't get enough rest?"

Julia nodded and rolled her eyes. "Most children are. It was okay when she was growing up, but she needs to snap out of it."

"She obviously never grew out of it. I think that some

people don't."

He studied Julia as she pondered his statement. Then she shook her head. "I think her problem reaches far beyond being tired. We all coddled her so much in the past that she thinks we should continue to do so."

"Sarah's not a bad person."

"I'm not saying she is," Julia said. "But she does expect certain things from us that no one can deliver, now that we have our own families."

"What can we do?"

Julia chuckled. "This is quite amusing."

"What?"

"You used to be the one I turned to for help, and now you're asking me what we can do."

John nodded. "That is because you have always been so good at making decisions. I trust your judgment."

Julia rose from her chair and went back over to the stove. "Unfortunately, I don't think this is anything that even the best judgment can fix. That is why I think you should go through with your marriage to Viola."

"But Sarah won't—"

"Sarah will have a choice," Julia said before he finished. "She can either continue being miserable or eventually accept the fact that you have your own life to live."

John understood what Julia was saying, and on some level he agreed. But he also knew that he would never marry anyone without his family's blessing. And that included everyone in his family.

"Are you staying for supper?" she asked.

He got up. "No, not tonight. I'll just eat some of the leftover ham and cornbread in the pantry."

"What would you like for me to tell Viola?"

"I'm right here, so if he needs to tell me something, he can do it now."

John glanced over toward the doorway and saw Viola standing there forcing a smile. "I've decided to eat in my cabin tonight." He paused before adding, "Alone."

He half expected her to look surprised or maybe even dismayed. But she didn't. Instead, she gave him an understanding smile and a brief nod. "That is fine. I was thinking I could do a little bit of knitting tonight anyway."

"Would you like some new yarn? We have some pretty colors at the store." He had an overwhelming urge to make things right with Viola since it appeared that there wouldn't be a wedding.

"Yes, that would be very nice, thank you."

"I'll buy some for you tomorrow. What colors do you prefer?"

Viola turned to Julia. "I thought I would make blankets for your children. What colors would they like?"

Now John felt even worse. This woman was selfless to a fault, and nothing that happened seemed to rattle her.

After he had a list of colors from Julia, he walked across the massive lawn toward his cabin. With this remorseful feeling burning a hole in his gut, he knew he would have a difficult time choking down even a small amount of dinner.

Chapter 4

Viola's heart ached for this hurting man who hadn't thought through the possible complications before he sent for her. She was pretty sure he wanted to go through with the wedding but that he wouldn't unless he had Sarah's blessing. His other daughters were fine with it, but Sarah clearly wasn't in favor of her father remarrying.

While Julia, Lenora, and Mary obviously thought that Sarah was acting spoiled and selfish, Viola suspected there was more to her actions. She'd seen it time after time— young mothers too harried to have clear, rational thoughts. Sure, she was probably still a little spoiled, being the youngest. But Viola could see through the outward signs of negativity to the pain she was obviously feeling.

Viola helped Julia get the children situated at the table before setting the table for the adults. During the meal, she hopped up when the children needed help so Julia could enjoy supper with her husband.

"I could get used to this," Julia said with a smile. "Maybe we can convince you to stick around for a while ... even if Papa—" A look of horror flashed across her face before she placed her hand over her own mouth. "I am so sorry."

"No, don't be. That's okay." Viola bent over and picked up a spoon that one of the children had dropped. "You don't have to worry about everything you say."

"I know. It's just that ..." Julia glanced over at Stone who had a look of amusement on his face. "We know that Papa wants to do the right thing. He really should have spent more time preparing Sarah before sending for you."

"But he didn't, and we can't change the past, can we?"

Julia shook her head. "You remind me a little of Mama. She was very wise."

"Of course she was. She married your father and raised four wonderful daughters." Viola decided it was time to change the subject. "Does your church do anything for Thanksgiving?"

"Why, yes, we do." Julia appeared relieved to change the subject. "Everyone bakes and brings food to the church. Since it is generally too cold to eat outdoors in November, we set up tables inside the church."

"I would like to bring something ..." Viola tilted her head. "That is, if I am still here."

Stone cleared his throat. "You may stay in our home as long as you like."

"Thank you."

"No," he said. "Thank you. I don't know if you realize how much you are helping out simply by entertaining the children with your stories."

Viola had always enjoyed storytelling. "Then I will continue doing it while I am here, as long as they are willing to listen."

*

Marvin was waiting for John at the general store when he arrived early. "We need to talk."

John saw the seriousness on his son-in-law's face and nodded. "Yes, of course. We have another half hour before the store opens."

"I am very concerned about Sarah," Marvin said. "She

doesn't talk much anymore, and she is always so worried about the baby. When I go in after a long day's work on the ranch, she is sometimes still sitting in the rocking chair, holding Abigail. I'm not even sure she puts her down during the day." Marvin ran his fingers through his hair. "It can't be good for Abigail, and it certainly isn't good for Sarah. She seems to have lost her spirit."

John nodded and thought about it for a moment. He remembered something Julia had told him about Viola. "Would you like for me to bring Viola over to help out?"

"I'm not so sure that would be a wise thing to do," Marvin said. "Sarah was already becoming overly protective of Abigail before Viola arrived, but after they met, the situation seems to have gotten worse."

"She's afraid I'm trying to replace her mama." John shoved his hands in his pockets and looked down at the floor. "But I can assure her that I won't do that. I would never marry someone my daughters don't approve of."

Marvin's jaw tightened. "Sarah has no right to tell you that you can't marry Viola."

"I know, but I would still want her blessing. Viola understands."

"Considering the circumstances, do you think Viola would even be willing to try to help?"

John nodded. "She is a good woman. I think she will."

Marvin lifted both hands before letting them fall back down to his sides. "I am willing to try anything to help my wife. It breaks my heart to see her in such a condition."

"I know. I feel the same way."

"Do you need any help in the store today? Henry said he would like more hours for the holidays."

"I can always use more help," John said. "We need to do inventory before we place our next order, so I would welcome the extra pair of hands."

"Thanks, John. Please let Viola know that I would appreciate anything she can do for Sarah."

After Marvin left, John gave himself a moment to ponder Sarah's reaction to Viola. He wasn't totally positive, but he was fairly certain that her reaction wasn't about Viola but more about her need to keep things as they always were.

Henry came in later that afternoon and got instructions on what was needed. He didn't seem to mind that John had changed the procedures since he was only able to work part-time. At the end of the day, John left knowing that they would be able to handle the busy holiday season.

Since he had something specific to discuss with Viola, he decided to do that before he went to his cabin. Again, she was perched on the front porch with Julia's children. They all ran up to him, gave him a hug, and went inside when he told them he needed some private time with their storyteller.

Viola smiled. "Julia and Stone's children are so delightful."

"I know. And you are so good with them. Too bad you didn't have some of your own."

The instant John said those words he regretted them. But she didn't even flinch. Instead, she nodded.

"I am about to ask you for a very large favor, and I will understand if you choose not to do it."

Viola didn't seem fazed. She just held his gaze and waited.

"Marvin came to talk to me today about Sarah." He shuffled his feet on the porch. "He is worried about her. Something has happened since she had Abigail, and it has only gotten worse with time."

"I can understand that."

"You can?"

"Yes. Something happens to a lot of women after they give birth. There are so many changes in their lives, and they don't know how to deal with them."

John nodded and blinked. "Do you think you can help her?"

"Is that the favor you're asking for?"

"Yes." He swallowed and braced himself for her rejection.

She glanced off into the distance before turning her attention back to him. "I will be happy to see what I can do. When would you like for me to start?"

"Is tomorrow too soon?"

"No, tomorrow is just fine. But I will need to discuss it with Julia so she won't expect me to help with the children here."

"I can stay out here with the children so you can go inside and talk to her."

*

Viola was surprised by the sense of urgency. John was clearly concerned about his daughter.

Julia glanced around at her as she entered the kitchen. "Where are the children?"

"Your father has them. He has asked me to talk to you about Sarah."

"Let me put this pan in the oven, and we can talk." Julia reached for a pan, slid it into the oven, closed the door, and dropped her towel on the counter. "Let's sit at the table."

As Viola explained what John had said, Julia listened attentively. After she finished, Julia spoke up. "I understand Papa being worried, but I'm not sure you're the person who should help her. After all, she sees you as the—" She gave an apologetic look.

"The enemy?" Viola said.

Julia sighed and nodded. "Yes, unfortunately, as long as she sees you as someone trying to take over Mama's place in the family, you won't be able to get through to her at all. I've known Sarah all her life, and she can be pretty stubborn."

"Then I will immediately let her know that I am not going to marry your father."

"I don't want you to lie," Julia said.

"That isn't a lie. I plan to go back home to Georgia as soon as there is no longer a chance of a winter storm."

"You do realize that could be months from now, right?"

"Yes."

Julia smiled. "I like the thought of having you here to help with the children through the winter. I hope you don't mind."

"I don't mind in the least."

"Well," Julia began, "since you won't be marrying Papa, there just might be a chance that she'll listen to you. What do you plan to say?"

"Probably not much. I would rather just go to her house and listen to her talk."

"Maybe that's what she needs." Julia turned toward the sound of the children shrieking as they ran into the house. "Sounds like Papa may have reached his limit."

"Mama, I'm hungry. When will supper be ready?"

Julia leaned over to face her oldest child. "It will be ready when it's ready. Why don't you find something to do while I finish cooking it?"

"I'll tell them another story," Viola said. "Come on, let's go back out to the porch."

Julia's children were easy to please. They all listened attentively as she told them one of her many stories about growing up in Georgia and how she used to play in the red clay. By the time Julia called them back into the kitchen, all of the children were ravenous.

*

The next morning, John came to get Viola to take her to Sarah's house. Marvin had agreed to open the store, and after John got Viola settled, he would head into town. And then Marvin would return home and take Viola back to Julia's house before he went to work on the ranch.

Sarah opened the door and hugged her father. Then she looked at Viola with that same vitriolic look she'd given her last time she'd seen her.

"What is *she* doing here?" Sarah asked.

"Don't talk like that," John said. "I brought her here to

help you out."

"I don't need help from her." Sarah pulled Abigail closer, turned her back, walked into the room, and sank down into the rocking chair.

"She is a beautiful baby," Viola said softly. "She looks like you."

As Sarah's jaw tightened, Viola saw the tears forming in her eyes. John clearly didn't know what to say or do next.

After several uncomfortable minutes, Viola turned to John. "Would you mind giving me a few minutes alone with Sarah?"

John glanced at his daughter, but before she had a chance to say a word, he turned and left the room. Viola sat on the edge of the settee with her hands folded in her lap.

"Sarah, I know that you don't approve of your father marrying me, which is why there will be no wedding." Viola licked her lips before continuing. "I plan to go back to Georgia as soon as the winter is over."

Sarah's chin lifted, but she still didn't say anything. Abigail made a gurgling sound.

"I have been helping Julia with her children, and I would like to help with Abigail while I'm still here."

"How can I believe you?" Sarah finally asked. "I don't know anything about you."

"What would you like to know?"

"I would still like to know why you would come all the way here to marry someone you've never met before."

Viola took a deep breath and slowly let it out as she tried to think of something to say that would satisfy Sarah. "You already asked me that when we first met, and I told you that I wanted a companion. But since there will be no wedding, I think that is a moot point."

"How do I know you are not here to hurt us?"

Viola lifted her eyebrows. "You don't."

"Are you?" Sarah shifted a little bit in her seat.

"Am I what?"

"Here to hurt us?"

Viola shook her head. "Think about what you just said, Sarah. If all I wanted to do was hurt someone, why would I come all this way? I could have done that back in Georgia."

Sarah's eyes fluttered closed before she opened them again and glanced back at Viola. "I would like some help."

Chapter 5

John stood outside on the porch, praying that something would change between his daughter and Viola. He had always tried so hard to be a decent father, but he knew he'd failed. After his wife passed away, everything in his life seemed to fall apart, and there didn't seem to be anything he could do to fix it ... at least not until Sarah's husband had given him the job at the general store.

Time seemed to drag by before Viola finally came out onto the porch. When he looked at her face, he saw her resignation.

"Is it bad?"

She pursed her lips and shook her head. "Not too bad."

"Do you want me to bring you back to Julia's house now?"

"No, I think I will stay here until Marvin can get back home."

"If you are sure that's what you want ..."

"I'm sure," Viola said. "Now go on into town so Marvin doesn't think something bad has happened."

Once John left, Viola turned around to go back into the house. She walked straight into the room where she'd left

Sarah and stopped at the door. The young woman was still sitting in the same chair holding the baby, staring at the wall, tears streaming down her cheeks.

Viola took a step closer, paused to gauge Sarah's reaction, and then took another couple of steps. "Sarah, dear, you look so exhausted. Would you like to take a nap?"

Sarah blinked and wiped her tears with the back of her hand. "I can't. Abigail will start crying."

"Will you allow me to hold her?" Viola asked as softly as she could.

"Does Julia let you hold her children?"

"Yes, in fact, I have been holding them and telling them story after story while Julia does her chores."

Sarah finally looked directly at Viola and nodded. "Yes, you may hold her ... but just for a little while and only if she doesn't cry."

"Why don't you take advantage of my being here and lie down for a little while? Marvin will be here soon, so you can rest until he gets here."

"I can't."

"Why not?" Viola glanced at the sweet baby's face and smiled. When Abigail grinned back at her, she showed Sarah. "See? She likes me. I think it will do her some good to get to know someone different, and she'll be much happier if you are rested."

"Only if you promise to come and get me if she starts crying."

"Yes, of course."

"Okay. My room is the second one on the right. I probably won't be able to sleep, but I would like to lie down for a little while."

"That's fine."

Once Sarah left the room, Viola focused all of her attention on Abigail, who gave her a big grin. "You are such a beautiful child."

Abigail cooed, making Viola laugh. And then Abigail

laughed.

Viola spent the next couple of hours singing to Abigail and walking around the house with her. She was such a happy child. She didn't exhibit any of the emotional problems Viola had seen in the children back home whose mothers were depressed after childbirth.

By the time she heard Marvin arrive, Viola felt as though she'd known this baby since the beginning. He smiled when he entered the house.

"Looks like you two are getting along quite well. Where is my wife?"

"She's resting," Viola said.

A look of concern crossed Marvin's face. "I hope she's not getting sick."

"I don't think she is," Viola said. "This is actually quite common after a woman gives birth. Have you had anyone come in to help her since Abigail was born?"

"People have offered, but she said she didn't want any help."

Viola smiled. "That's part of the problem. Giving birth is exhausting, and a woman needs plenty of rest afterward. Maybe I can come over a couple of days a week until I leave."

Marvin gave her a long look of appreciation. "That will be nice … if she lets you."

"Why don't you check on her before you take me back to Julia's place?"

As soon as Marvin went to check on Sarah, Viola went into the kitchen and started washing the dishes that had piled up. It looked like Sarah didn't do much besides hold her baby all day. She had just finished rinsing the last plate when she heard a noise behind her. She turned around and saw Sarah standing by the door looking as though she had just awakened.

"Did you get enough rest?" Viola asked.

Sarah didn't respond. Instead, she took a few steps closer.

"Marvin said you want to come by every now and then."

"That is correct."

"Can you come back tomorrow?"

"Is that what you want?" Viola asked.

Sarah glanced down before lifting her gaze to meet Viola's. "Yes."

Viola had to clear her throat to keep Sarah from hearing the surprise in her voice. "I'll see if your father can bring me here before he leaves for work in the morning."

The sound of Abigail crying from the blanket on the floor caught Sarah's attention. She turned, picked up the baby, and without another word, left Viola standing there alone.

*

As soon as Marvin dropped Viola off at Julia's house, the children ran toward her. Julia laughed.

"Looks like you are the popular person around here," Julia said.

Viola laughed. "That is only because I am their fun person. I don't have any expectations or make any demands the way a parent would."

Julia gave her a look of appreciation. "Very much like a grandmother."

"Yes." Viola didn't want Julia to think she was trying to replace her mother, so she added, "However, I am simply a temporary guest, so I suppose I should keep some distance."

She looked at the littlest child with her arms stretched upward. There was no way she could resist such a sweet face, so she bent over and picked her up.

Julia laughed. "Will that be possible? They are already attached to you."

The remainder of the day, Viola played with the children, sang songs with them, and helped Julia with the housework when the little ones took a nap. She knew she was creating a deeper relationship with John's daughter's family than she should have, considering the fact that she would be leaving as soon as it warmed up enough.

*

All the way home from work, John prayed for guidance. Although he had already decided to send Viola back to Georgia, he was having some doubts. From the moment they'd met, he liked everything about her—from the way she looked to her easy laughter. He admired her for her ability to so quickly warm up to his grandchildren. And now that he knew Viola was here, he looked forward to the end of the workday when he could see her. The very thought of Sarah's reaction sent a shiver of annoyance through him.

John pulled up in front of Julia's house in time to see Viola playing a lawn game with the children. The vision before him warmed his heart in a way he never expected in the beginning. This woman was truly a gem—one he wished he never had to let go.

And then she looked at him. The instant their gazes met, his insides went weak. There was something in her glance— a familiarity and understanding that said more than words ever could—that turned him inside out. He wanted her now more than ever.

Any woman who had the ability to command respect and gain the adoration of these children as quickly as Viola could was one who needed to be given a chance. He couldn't allow Sarah's attitude to interfere with a relationship that he now had no doubt was his gift from God, after all the years of suffering and loneliness.

He had to find a way to keep Viola here in Colorado. Now, more than ever, he wanted to make her his wife.

"How was your day at the store?" Viola asked. "Were you busy?"

He pulled a bag from the floor of the carriage. "Not too busy to get some yarn. I hope you like these colors."

Viola's eyes sparkled with delight as he handed her the bag. She peeked inside before returning his gaze. "They're beautiful. I love them."

It had been years since he'd been able to make a woman

look at him like that, and it felt mighty good. He lifted his head and squared his shoulders. "Let me know when you need more."

Viola reached for the hand of the nearest child. "Come on, children, let's get cleaned up for supper. I'm sure your mother is almost finished cooking."

John watched as all of Julia's little ones did as they were told. He pondered saying something to her about his thoughts, but he decided it would be best to wait until later after the children went to bed.

But as the evening wore on, he saw that the opportunity wasn't going to present itself ... at least not yet. As eager as he was to talk to her, he knew it would be best to wait.

*

The next morning, Viola sat up in bed and rubbed her eyes before standing and walking over to the vanity. She was starting to enjoy Colorado—so much so that she knew she would miss it after she left. Julia's family was delightful, but what brought a deep joy to her heart was seeing John when he got home from work most days.

When she first agreed to become a mail order bride, she never expected to fall in love so quickly. Now that their plans had been thwarted, she knew that her heart belonged to John, and it would be broken when she left. The irony of the situation saddened her.

Julia and the children greeted her when she walked into the kitchen. "They've been wanting to wake you up ever since the crack of dawn." Julia laughed. "They love you."

A lump formed in Viola's throat as she looked around at the children who had a big piece of her heart. "They are precious gifts from God."

Julia slowly turned around to face her. "There is another gift from God that we can't ignore." She pursed her lips.

"And what is that?" Viola asked.

"The love you and Papa are starting to feel for each other."

"I-I …" Viola cast her gaze downward. She couldn't deny what Julia had said, but she also couldn't see the point in dwelling on it.

"You simply cannot leave Colorado."

"But Sarah—"

"Look, Viola, Sarah is a grown woman with her own family. She loved our mother just like we all did. But Mama has been gone for quite a while now, so we need to think about what is best for Papa." She paused and sighed. "And I think that you can make him happy."

"I would never want to cause a rift."

"You are not causing a rift. Lenora and I spoke yesterday. She brought her children over to play with their cousins while you were at Sarah's house. She agrees with me—that seeing a smile on Papa's face when you're around is more important than one of Sarah's spoiled fits."

Viola thought for a moment. "I'm not so sure that's what this is about."

"What are you talking about?"

"Think about it, Julia. Sarah has always been pampered, but just a couple of years ago, she was thrust into the position of having to grow up and become a wife. Granted, she has her father and all of her sisters nearby, but it's still different since you are all busy with your families."

Julia nodded. "But she knows we're here for her whenever she needs us."

"Yes, but then she had a baby. That alone has sent many sane women over the edge." Viola smiled. "I've seen it before. Babies are demanding and can cause many sleepless nights."

"That is true. I remember when my first child came along. I wasn't sure what hit me."

"Add that to the fact that Sarah has no experience with younger children since she is the baby of your family, and you have a recipe for frustration."

Julia tilted her head and gazed admiringly at Viola. "Such

wisdom."

"As I said last time you told me that, I have seen quite a bit." She heard a carriage approaching. "I need to grab something quick to eat. Sarah is expecting me."

Chapter 6

John helped Viola into the carriage before going around to his side. Viola could tell he had something on his mind.

"Do you have some news?" she asked.

"What do you mean?" He tightened his grip on the reins before turning to look at her.

"You look like one of the children who can't wait to share something."

His smile widened. "We can talk about it later. So how did you sleep last night?"

"Very well. It is so quiet and restful here."

"I take it you like Colorado."

She nodded. "Yes, I like it very much."

"Good." He turned his attention to the road.

"I hope Sarah feels better today." She folded her hands on her lap. "The poor girl looked as though she hadn't slept in weeks."

"If she could ever make herself put Abigail down, she might be able to rest."

Viola sighed. "I am sure she just wants to do the right thing. Have you ever thought that the problem might be that she doesn't know what to do with a small child?"

"I thought—" He stopped for a moment. "I am sure it's not easy."

They rode along in silence for a few minutes, giving Viola time to think about what she would do with Sarah and Abigail today. First, she'd have to observe and evaluate Sarah's mood.

They pulled up in front of the house, where John got out to help Viola to the door. He knocked, and as soon as Sarah hollered, "Come on in," he opened it.

"Would you like for me to stay a while?" he asked.

She shook her head. "No, I can handle this. But thank you." The look of concern on his face warmed her heart. She placed her hand on his shoulder. "We will be just fine."

Sarah still hadn't come out from the back of the house when John left, so Viola went to the kitchen to start a kettle of water for some tea. Then she went to check on Sarah and the baby.

She found them in the baby's room that had a crib, a small dresser, and a rocking chair, where Sarah sat, holding Abigail. The baby turned to Viola and grinned.

Viola walked toward them and gave Sarah a questioning look. "May I hold her?"

After only a brief hesitation, Sarah nodded and handed Abigail to Viola. "Just for a little while. I'll take her back when she starts crying."

From the look on the baby's face, it didn't appear that there would be any crying—at least not any time soon. Abigail let out a shriek of joy as Viola grinned at her. Sarah groaned and held her stomach.

"Are you not feeling well?" Viola asked. "When was the last time you had something to eat?"

"A couple of days ago."

The teakettle started to whistle, so Viola urged Sarah to go to the kitchen with her. "Why don't I fix you some toast to go with your tea?"

Viola was surprised that Sarah allowed her to take over in

the kitchen. She held her daughter while Viola prepared a plate with toast and jam and a cup of tea with honey and lemon. Then Viola took Abigail so Sarah could eat.

With each bite, a little bit of color returned to Sarah's cheeks. Finally, she let out a sigh of satisfaction. "That was good."

Abigail reached out and yanked on a stray strand of hair that had fallen from Viola's clip. Then she laughed.

Viola glanced at Sarah who looked horrified before turning back to Abigail. "You silly girl. Do you want some of my hair for your bald head?"

Abigail laughed. And then she reached for Viola's hair again.

"No, Abigail!" Sarah started to get up.

"She's fine," Viola said. "Please try to relax, Sarah. This is what babies do."

Sarah sank back in her chair and hung her head. "I'm afraid that I knew nothing about babies before I had Abigail." She sighed. "And I still don't know much."

"Why don't we put these dishes in the sink and go into the other room where we can relax a bit more?" Viola handed Abigail back to Sarah so she could clear the table. "I can wash the dishes later."

Once as they got to the front room, Viola placed a blanket on the floor and put Abigail on it. Sarah started to grab her, but Viola held up her hands.

"She needs a little bit of floor time so she can learn to crawl. Most babies do that before they walk, you know."

"Oh." Sarah sat back and stared at Abigail. "I didn't know that."

"Now you do."

"I am probably the worst mama you have ever seen." Sarah's voice cracked.

Viola watched Abigail for a few seconds before turning back to Sarah. "Babies are actually quite resilient little creatures. Mamas all make mistakes, but the babies somehow manage to survive."

Sarah blinked a few times before wiping a tear that had escaped. "I'm sure I've made more than my share of mistakes with her."

"Of course you have. But that's how you learn. Abigail knows you love her."

At the sound of her name, Abigail looked at her mother and started to whimper. Sarah jumped up and reached for her.

"Why don't you sit back down?" Viola said.

"But she's about to start crying."

"That's another thing babies need to do. She needs to learn that there are other people in the world besides her. If she cries to be held, it is fine to pick her up. But give her a little bit of time first. You might discover that she can find something else to make her happy."

Viola picked up a ragdoll from the table and placed it on the floor beside the baby. Abigail smiled up at Viola before picking up the doll and grinning at it.

"See?"

Sarah watched her daughter and then looked at Viola. "I didn't know."

"Another thing you might want to start thinking about is letting her know what is or isn't allowed. If you start early, it will be much easier as she gets older."

Sarah nodded. "Okay."

"Why don't you go in your bedroom and rest? I'll keep Abigail occupied until dinnertime."

Without a word, Sarah stood and left the room. Abigail didn't even realize her mother had left the room.

*

"You really care about this woman, don't you?" Marvin stood on the other side of the counter, perusing the candy selection.

"I do."

Marvin laughed. "I bet you didn't expect it either."

"You're right." John wanted more than anything to talk about his feelings for Viola, but he didn't think it would be right to discuss her with his son-in-law since Sarah was the one who stood in his way.

"I hope you are aware that Sarah is starting to soften to Viola."

John blinked. "She is? Did she tell you that?"

"Not in so many words, but I can tell. In fact, this morning, when we first woke up, she asked if Viola was still coming over." Marvin's voice softened. "For the first time since Abigail was born, I'm starting to see some of the old Sarah, and I think Viola might be responsible for that."

"Perhaps Sarah is being nice because Viola and I have decided not to marry."

"Maybe …" Marvin picked up a chocolate bar and put it on the counter before pulling a coin from his pocket. "But I won't be surprised if we see a major change in her attitude."

John pondered that and then nodded. "That would be nice, but I'm not holding my breath."

Marvin unwrapped his candy and extended it to John. "Would you like a piece before I bite into it?"

"No thanks."

After Marvin finished his candy, he headed toward the door. "I have quite a bit to do around the ranch today to get ready for the cattle I bought last weekend. I'll take Viola back to Julia's house after dinner."

John rocked back on his heels and surveyed the store. He loved his life here. The only thing that would make his life better was if Sarah could accept Viola as his wife.

*

When Marvin arrived, Abigail squealed with delight at the sight of her father. Viola laughed.

"Something smells mighty good," Marvin said as he picked his daughter up off the blanket on the floor, walked over to the stove, and glanced in the pots. "Where is Sarah?"

"She has been resting all morning."

He lifted an eyebrow. "I'm surprised. Does she know that you put Abigail down?"

Viola nodded. "Yes, in fact, she and I had a talk about that before her rest. I explained that babies need a little bit of floor time so they can learn to crawl and then walk."

"How do you know so much about babies, Viola?"

She clasped her hands in front of her and smiled. "I have taken care of many women who were exhausted after childbirth. My folks made sure I would never need to work, so I had time after they passed away to help people from church when they needed an extra pair of hands."

"Your hands have been a blessing for us around here," Marvin said.

"They sure have."

The sound of Sarah's voice in the doorway grabbed Viola and Marvin's attention. They both glanced in her direction as she stood there surveying the situation. Abigail screeched and extended her arms in Sarah's direction.

As Sarah walked over to take the baby from Marvin's arms, she cast a brief smile in Viola's direction. "Thank you so much for helping me out. I feel better than I have in a very long time."

Viola let out a deep sigh of relief. She wasn't sure how Sarah would feel when she came out after her rest.

Abigail reached for Sarah's hair and gave it a hearty yank. Viola held her breath until she saw a smile form on Sarah's lips.

"You are such a squirt!" She tilted Abigail's face up to hers. "Don't pull hair, Abigail. That hurts."

The baby's chin quivered at the sternness of Sarah's voice, making Viola wonder what Sarah would do next. To her delight, she pulled the baby close to her chest and just swayed back and forth until Abigail relaxed.

As they ate dinner a few minutes later, Viola talked about some of Abigail's antics. Sarah and Marvin laughed and exchanged loving glances, letting Viola know that everything was much better between them.

*

The hustle and bustle of Thanksgiving came and went. Viola loved all of the activities, but she was glad when things calmed down. The Christmas season was much more relaxing.

She had fallen into a comfortable routine of visiting Sarah a couple of days a week. At first, she took care of Abigail while Sarah rested, but as time went on, the two of them spent more time talking about child rearing and housework. Viola was surprised to learn that no one had actually made Sarah learn some basic cooking and cleaning skills, so she took it upon herself to teach her.

"This is much easier than I realized," Sarah said as she prepared her first pot of stew. "I always thought it was more complicated."

"Isn't that how it usually is?" Viola pulled some flour from the pantry. "Next time I come, I'll teach you how to make a very easy but flaky pie crust."

She set the flour on the counter and turned around to check on Sarah. To her surprise, Sarah had her arms folded, her head tilted to one side, and a grin on her lips.

"Did I say something funny?"

Sarah shook her head. "No, but I have something to tell you."

"What is that?"

"I want you to marry my father."

"You what?"

Sarah laughed. "I think you heard me. Viola, you are probably one of the best things that have happened to my family since Mama died. And I know he still wants to marry you."

Viola's throat constricted. John had already told her he wanted to marry her, even if Sarah never came around. She had stood firm, though, and said she had changed her mind and wanted to go back to Georgia in the spring.

"What if I don't want to marry him?" Viola countered.

All of the color quickly faded from Sarah's face. "But—"

Viola held up a hand. "Whatever your father and I do is between him and me. But I certainly appreciate your kind words. It's nice to know that you don't hate me."

Sarah lowered her head and shook it. "I never hated you. I was just being selfish."

"No, you weren't being selfish. You were just afraid and confused ... and exhausted to the point of not thinking straight."

Sarah lifted her gaze and looked Viola in the eyes. "Is there any way I can get you to change your mind about marrying Papa?"

Chapter 7

A week before Christmas, John walked up and down the holiday aisle at the store, searching for just the right ornament to give Viola. Sarah had spoken with him and told him what she'd said to Viola. She'd also told him that Viola was the one being stubborn now.

She might be stubborn, he thought, but he planned to do everything in his power to change her mind. He'd grown to love her as had his daughters, and now he couldn't imagine their lives without her.

He finally found a red ornament that glistened as it turned. It would look beautiful on the tree in the cabin he would share with Viola if she would agree to marry him soon.

After his talk with Sarah, all of his daughters had come together with a plan to help convince Viola to stay in Colorado. He wasn't sure if the plan would work, but if she had the slightest desire to stick around, it just might.

Viola was with Sarah today, and he had agreed to pick her up on his way home from the store. The days were shorter, so it was dark by the time he turned the closed sign.

He pulled the carriage up to the front of Sarah's house,

got out, and went up to the door. Viola opened it before he knocked.

"I heard you coming," she explained. "We got Abigail to go to sleep early, so I thought you and I could scoot on out of here so Sarah and Marvin could have some time to themselves."

John smiled and nodded. "Then let's go."

All the way home, John's mind raced with his plan. The girls had convinced him that he should propose in the privacy of his cabin to give them a chance to discuss any concerns about them. And then they'd all be waiting at Julia's house to celebrate.

When he made the turn toward the cabin, Viola gave him a curious look. "I'm tired, John. I'd really like to go to Julia's."

His hands shook as he smiled at her in the moonlight. "There is just one thing I would like to do first. It won't take long." He reached for her hand and squeezed it. "I promise."

Viola was too nice to say no, something he had counted on. He pulled up in front of the cabin, helped her out, picked up the bag with the ornament, and guided her toward the door.

"Did you leave something burning?" she asked as they approached the cabin.

He had asked Julia to stop by and light a candle so they wouldn't come home to an empty house. "I think my daughter might have done that so her old papa wouldn't trip over something in the dark."

Viola laughed. "Her old papa is one of the most nimble men I have ever known. I can't see you tripping over anything."

"You haven't seen me in the dark." He opened the door and gestured inside where a fire was burning in the fireplace, and the aroma of gingerbread filled the cabin. "Want some cake?"

"Before dinner?"

He laughed. "Let's be naughty and have dessert first."

Her smile warmed his heart as she nodded. "Just don't tell the children."

He pulled a couple of dishes from the cabinet, placed them on the table, and lifted the lid off the cake platter. As they ate, they talked about their day. Finally, he took the plates to the sink and ushered her over to the sofa.

"In case you were wondering, this was all planned. I have something very important to discuss with you." He took her hand in his and looked into her eyes. "I know that I sent for you as a sight-unseen mail order bride. I didn't know if I would love you, but I knew that I wanted companionship."

She nodded. "Yes, I understand that."

"But something happened along the way." He grinned and squeezed her hand. "I fell in love with you."

Her eyes widened. She opened her mouth, but nothing came out.

So he took advantage of her speechlessness and picked up the ornament. "I have a present for you." Then he handed it to her.

As she opened it, she smiled. "This is lovely, John."

"I know, and I would like for it to be the first ornament on our tree." He gestured toward the small, bare tree in the corner of the room. "That is, if you will agree to marry me."

"Are you sure? What about your girls? What about Sarah?"

"We have their blessing ... even Sarah's. Now the only person I'm not sure about is you." He glanced at the ornament and then into her eyes. "If you don't want to marry me, I understand. You can take that back to Georgia to remember your time in Colorado. But if you—"

Before he had a chance to finish his sentence, Viola stood and walked over to the tree. She looked it over and then finally chose a spot where she hung the ornament. When she turned around, he saw the smile that covered her face.

"Does this mean—?"

She nodded. "Yes, John, I will marry you."

He pulled her into his arms and gave her a big kiss. "I've been wanting to do that for a long time."

"And I've been wanting you to."

"Now we have to do something else." He took her by the hand and led her back outside. "The girls and their husbands are all waiting at Julia and Stone's house to celebrate."

Epilogue

On Christmas Eve, Viola and John said their vows in front of his four daughters, their husbands, and all of his grandchildren. After he placed the ring on her finger, they turned around to face the family.

Within seconds, everyone had joined them at the front of the church and crowded around the couple for hugs. Viola couldn't remember a time when she'd been so happy.

She had come to Colorado to marry a companion, and now she was happy to have discovered the man she loved with all her heart. His family was a bonus she'd never expected.

After everyone hugged her, Sarah approached with a sheepish look on her face. "Marvin and I were wondering something." She glanced over her shoulder at her husband, and he nodded before she turned back to Viola. "We wanted to know if it's okay for Abigail to call you Granny Vi."

Viola's heart melted. "I would be honored for her to call me that."

Julia came up from behind. "That's a relief. Mary, Lenora, and I have been telling the children that they're all to call you that."

John tugged on her hand. "Come on, Viola. It's time for

us to start being husband and wife." He waved to his daughters. "We will see the rest of you later."

As soon as they got into the carriage, he pulled her into his arms and kissed her. "Will I always have to compete with my daughters for your time?"

"No, never. You will always come first."

"Okay, then, now that we have that settled, let's go home to *our* cabin."

I hope you enjoyed the *Hollister Sisters Mail Order Bride* series collection. Please don't forget to leave a review.

Thank you!
Debby Mayne
www.debbymayne.com

Printed in Great Britain
by Amazon